I0579612

READER PRAISE FOR THE ESSIEN SERIES

"A real page turner"

"Love the Essien family"

"My new favourite author"

"Excellent"

"Great series"

"Fantastic"

"I want to be like Felix Essien when I grow up!"

ALSO BY KIRU TAYE

The Essien Series
Keeping Secrets
Making Scandal
Riding Rebel
Kola
A Very Essien Christmas
Freddie Entangled
Freddie Untangled

Bound Series
Bound to Fate
Bound to Ransom
Bound to Passion
Bound to Favor
Bound to Liberty

The Challenge Series
Valentine
Engaged
Worthy
Captive

Passion Shields Series
Scars
Secrets
Scores

Men of Valor Series
His Treasure
His Strength
His Princess

Others
Haunted
Outcast
Sacrifice
Black Soul

Making SCANDAL

First Published in Great Britain in 2018 by
LOVE AFRICA PRESS
103 Reaver House, 12 East Street, Epsom KT17 1HX
www.loveafricapress.com

Text copyright © Kiru Taye, 2014

All rights reserved.
No part of this publication may be reproduced, stored
or transmitted in any form by any means, electronic,
mechanical, photocopying or otherwise, without the prior
permission of the publisher, except in the case of brief
quotations embodied in reviews.

The right of Kiru Taye to be identified as author of
this work has been asserted by them in accordance with the
Copyright, Design and Patents Act, 1988

This is a work of fiction. Names, places, events and
incidents are either the products of the author's imagination
or used fictitiously. Any resemblance to actual persons,
living or dead, is purely coincidental.

ISBN: 978-1-9164755-3-3
Also available as ebook and audiobook

DEDICATION

To Chioma Nwoko Adeshina, I miss you.

There is nothing better than someone
who derives joy from having you in their life
who treasures you even in the small things
who welcomes you when times are hard
who consoles you when you are down
and who loves you no matter what.

PROLOGUE

Mark Essien strode down the empty aisle towards the boxing ring. On his left hand side marched Felix, his older brother, Kola Banks, their bodyguard, on the man's other side. His brother's pace, controlled and confident, belied the rush of adrenaline pumping through his veins.

Mark knew. Anyone who saw Felix in his blue-with-white-band boxing attire—boots, shorts, robe and gloves—and understood what lay ahead would be clued in too.

Boxing had never been Mark's thing, but Felix enjoyed it as a sport. Apart from training sessions at the membership-by-invitation-only exclusive private gym they used to keep in shape, he had not participated in a boxing fight since his days at university.

Footsteps echoed off the hard flooring, announcing their arrival with the thud of insistent drumbeats. Musk and citrus from air fresheners scented the cool air, wafting from overhead air-conditioning units. Beyond the reach of the aisle spotlights, the rest of the area lay in darkness, the spaced out exercise equipment resembling misshapen, shadowed aliens.

A touch of unease tightened Mark's shoulders. This would be Felix's first serious match since his car accident and the subsequent six-week coma. Had four months been enough for him to recover?

Foolhardy notion to box today. However, no amount of logic from Mark convinced his brother to not fight. Good or bad, determination ran in Essien blood, a trait they all shared and part of the reason their business ventures rocketed with successes.

However, Felix had a wife, Ebony, and a baby on the way; no harm should come to him. They might not share the same mother, but Felix was his brother; his blood. And Essiens stood side by side, in love *and* in war.

Like right now.

In the ring occupying a chunk of the massive well-kitted gymnasium, his brother's opponent leaned against the ropes, his corner men on either side of him. The referee stood at the centre alongside the owner of the boxing club. No one loitered in the sidelines. Kola had arranged this strictly private affair to set things right for Felix.

A lesson needed to be taught. No man messed with an Essien and got away with it.

Kola parted the ropes and Felix stepped between them. Mark stood at the edge of the ring, his hands in his trouser pockets, projecting outward calm when inside his concern for his brother's wellbeing rose. His stomach churned and his mouth dried out. He eyed the cooler at the base of the square platform which contained plastic bottles of mineral water, but didn't pick any.

Felix gave a cursory nod in acknowledgement at the other man. His opponent pulled his lips back, baring blue gum shield in a nasty sneer. This wasn't meant to be a friendly fight. The stakes were too high, almost a winner takes all.

Felix ignored the man's taunt and rolled his shoulders, hopping around on his corner of the ring to keep his heart rate up.

Mark squinted at the opponent jumping and pacing his half of the ring. Stocky, he packed more weight than Felix, so if his brother got hit, he'd feel it. Felix had religiously watched all those videos of Mohammed Ali fights as a teenager. He hoped his sibling had learned a thing or two about avoiding punches.

"Float like a butterfly, sting like a bee," would come in very handy today.

The referee introduced them—Felix Essien versus Dele Savage—read out the rules, and started the countdown to the first round.

Kola took Felix's robe and stepped out of the ring. "Remember, keep moving. Don't let him hit you."

Felix jabbed the air in quick succession, hopped twice, and turned. Mark caught his gaze, leaned onto the hard base below the last rope and said, "Knock him the fuck out."

His brother nodded, bared the white mouth-guard in a grin, and rotated to face his adversary. At the bell, Dele Savage lived true to his name and ran at his brother like a bull, with a jab. Felix ducked and hit out with a left hook, connecting with his opponent's right side. They circled each other. Another jab came at him. He blocked and threw a cross punch.

Watching his brother fight reminded Mark of the first time he'd ever seen Felix throw a punch. As a kid, Mark had been thin and tall, bookish and a little awkward. His confidence and body had filled out later, in his teenage years.

In his earlier days, he'd lived with his mother who hadn't been married to Chief Essien, their father at the time. He'd known Felix was his older brother by two years, though they lived in different homes yet attended the same primary school.

Felix has always been athletic, at home on the sports field. Mark preferred playing a Gameboy or reading a book than doing anything that required physical exertion.

In those days, Mark couldn't understand why he only saw his brother at school, or why they couldn't hang out more frequently. Neither did he understand why he could only see his father once a month.

The kids in his school picked up on this fact and made fun of him. Mark had hated the taunts and lashed out the only way he could, with his acerbic tongue. One lad hadn't taken his blistering words well and had gone as far as pushing him down in the playground.

Like a super hero, Felix had stepped in and asked the kid to back off. Between the heart hammering in his chest and the loud rush of blood in his ears, Mark could barely open his mouth to tell his brother not to defend him. After all, Bully Bami, as the boy was known by the pupils, was twice the size of most kids in the playground and Felix went on a suicide mission by challenging him.

Still, Mark could only watch on as if the actions unfolding before him were from a television screen. The boy shoved Felix in the chest. Felix responded with a jab that landed midriff and sent Bami careening into the circle of kids and onto his backside.

The incident earned them a trip to the Headmaster's office and an earful from their father. But Felix and Mark's relationship had been cemented on that day. Mark developed an awe-like respect for his older brother. When Felix's mother passed on and Mark's father married his mother, they all lived under the same roof, finally, and Mark and Felix became almost inseparable.

Ding. The sound of the bell drew his attention back to his surroundings. The first round ended. Felix stepped back and lowered his body onto the stool Kola placed in his corner.

The bodyguard bounded into the ring and crouched over Felix, outlining Dele's weaknesses and what Felix needed to do, while Mark pulled himself up behind the ropes and rubbed his brother's shoulders, reinforcing his silent presence with the physical contact. Mark's strength didn't manifest in the technicalities of boxing. But his brother would feel his presence and know that Mark stood behind him, with him, in this and always.

The next round went great and quickly. All of Felix's punches hit their mark and he avoided being hit, except for one glancing blow on his shoulder.

In the third round, he caught the man out with a right upper cut, blood flying in the air. A drop splattered on Felix's forehead. Dele hit the deck. The dull, satisfying thud reminded Mark of sacks of food being offloaded out of containers at Apapa Wharf and chucked into mountainous piles.

The bell rang. Air rushed out of Mark's mouth, the tension knotting his muscles dissipating. Not that he hadn't believed in his brother winning the match. He just didn't like watching Felix get hurt.

Moreover he'd never witnessed Felix lose a fight except to Kola. Then again, they were not in the same class. It would be like comparing limes and oranges—Felix's welterweight to Kola's super middleweight. As a former member of the Nigerian Armed Forces, Kola was a trained fighter, built like a bullet-proof armoured tanker, but with the reflexes of a stealth fighter jet.

Kola jumped over the ropes and parted them for Mark to step through. Lips curled in a full smile, Mark embraced Felix, not caring that his torso was slick with sweat and wet patches now stained Mark's blue, silk shirt. Kola patted Felix's face with a towel.

The referee stepped forward and grabbed Felix's hand, lifting it high above their heads as he declared the winner.

Now, to collect the prize.

When Kola's investigation had pointed all fingers at Ebony's ex-fiancé as the man who had taped his encounter with her and sold it on to the blackmailer, Felix, Kola, and Mark had agreed they needed to get back at Mr. Savage. Kola had wanted to throw the man to the wolves or the *area boys,* the local gang of men Kola had mixed with as a kid, who saw Dele's actions as an affront to one of them.

But Felix hadn't wanted a street brawl.

Neither had Mark. He had learned early in life that he could cause as much harm to a person with his brain as with a fist. In those days, what he lacked in superior athletic skill, he more than made up in academic prowess. He learned to read people and understand what made them tick.

One valuable lesson he acquired—people were willing to pay whatever price for an easier life.

So he started charging to do students' homework and tutoring them. Since he was in a private school, all the kids there were from wealthy families, so pocket money was par for the course. By the time he got to secondary school, he hadn't needed the pocket money from his parents. He had a regular income.

So when it came to punishing Dele, Mark's suggestion had been to strip the man of what made him a man—his wealth. Take away his job, house, and car, and make him destitute. This was Africa, after all. And like it or not, a man's worth was measured mostly by his status and lifestyle. Take them away and he would cease to be relevant in society and become nothing. Nobody.

Felix had chosen the boxing ring, instead—a legal and equally painful option—and had thrown the challenge to Dele in a way he couldn't resist. Enter the boxing ring with Felix or face a malpractice suit. And of course, Dele hadn't known his opponent had been an Olympic standard athlete in his prime. Their family home had a cabinet decorated with Felix's tournament trophies.

To Felix, challenging Mr. Savage to a boxing match was the equivalent of a duel, an arrangement to engage into combat between two individuals to preserve one or the other's honour. Not only had Dele betrayed Ebony's trust, he had insulted Felix, in the process.

And according to his brother, "there's no greater satisfaction than the impact and crunch against flesh and bones when you knock an opponent out and see him sprawled on the floor."

Now the rat rocked on his knees before Mark's brother, his face and lips distended from Felix's punches. Kola slipped a smart phone into Felix's hand, the small white towel now hanging over Felix's shoulders.

"I warned you that if you messed with my wife, I'd make you pay for it. You should've heeded my advice," Felix said, his voice raspy from the aftermath of his fight, his chest heaving as he inhaled short breaths.

"I haven't seen or spoken to your wife since that day in the hospital," Dele mumbled through swollen lips, his head bent, his shoulders slumped.

Felix squatted beside his beaten foe. "I believe you. However, pictures of you and my wife were sent to me and my father with a threat of it being published online if we don't meet specific demands. Do you know anything about that?"

"No. I...I don't."

"We'll see. Kindly unlock your phone for me." He held out the phone so Dele could see it.

"I won't. Why should I?" The man lifted his head and glared with defiance, spitting a wad of bloody saliva at Felix's feet.

Kola stepped forward.

Felix appeared to retain his cool, though. "You might consider changing your mind. Unlike me, Kola here has no qualms about disfiguring this pretty face of yours. No woman would want to look at it ever again."

Dele's eyes widened and he pushed off the floor with his hands and staggered backward. Kola bunched his fists and took another step forward.

"All right. The code is 9-3-2-9."

"Thank you." Felix entered the number to the phone keypad and unlocked the screen. He accessed the media folder and scrolled through until he found what he was looking for.

"Well, well, well. So it *was* you. You recorded your time with Ebony and sold it on to a blackmailer. What kind of man are you?"

Disgust rolled through Mark and bile touched the back of his throat. What kind of bastard set up the woman who had once loved him?

"Tell me the name of the man," Felix ordered in a soft tone.

"No. I can't," Dele replied, shaking his head.

Felix nodded.

Kola threw a jab and Dele fell back into the corner of the ring. He lifted his arms to block and punch back, but Kola didn't let up. Each of his punches connected, the pounding sound against flesh and bones reverberating in the space, mixing in with Dele's grunts.

None of the other men in the gym intervened. Not even Dele's corner men. They stood behind the ropes, watching as Kola delivered his own brand of justice and torture.

"Just say the name and he will stop," Mark's brother added after a moment.

"Petersen," Dele shouted in a pained voice. "Kris Petersen paid me to give him information about you and your wife."

Kola stopped throwing punches and stepped back. Felix nodded and gave the phone to Mark.

He opened the back and removed the micro SD card, then threw the phone on the floor where it shattered into pieces. They would retain the evidence and this way, Dele couldn't cause any more damage with those photos.

Dele's supporters suddenly turned up at his side, pulling him up from his slumped position. He shook them off, the snarl on his cut lips broadcasting his displeasure as well as the angry words he spat out in Yoruba.

"My promise still stands. Keep away from my wife so you can live a long life. I won't be so gentlemanly next time."

Felix stepped off the ring and walked out, with Mark and Kola behind.

Kris Petersen – Nil. The Essiens – One.

The fight had only just begun.

CHAPTER ONE

Six months earlier...

"How can one man be so damned good-looking?"

Faith Brown tapped away on the screen of her hand-held tablet, ignoring Stella Orovi's provocative statement. Her friend placed two tall glasses of the drinks she'd just ordered onto paper coasters and bumped the table as she sat down. Not wanting any liquid splashed onto her device, Faith grabbed it and raised her head, flashing a warning glance before returning to her task.

"Don't tell me you're not interested. He is one of the hottest men alive."

Stella's sweet and insistent voice drew her attention again.

"Do I look like I care?" Her tone came out short and snappy. She would rather concentrate on the email message she was typing out than give in to the temptation of her friend's words.

"You do realise this is supposed to be a party and we're supposed to be letting our hair down for the night," Stella muttered, raising the glass of what looked like vodka and coke to her lips and taking a large sip.

Blowing out air through her mouth, Faith lifted her head. "I'm sorry. I'll get in a party mood once I finish what I'm doing. I have to reply these emails before I can relax."

"It's Friday evening. I'm sure everyone in Lagos is preparing to go home or has already left for the weekend. And we're in Jo'burg. Those emails can wait till Monday." Stella flicked her manicured hand at the gadget on the dark wood tabletop and leaned back into her oxblood leather sofa, her gaze sweeping the bar lounge.

"They can't," Faith huffed out, rolled her stiff shoulders and returned to her emails. Around her, people's conversations hummed and low music piped out of hidden speakers. She filtered out the sounds and concentrated on finishing her task.

One of those people who could never put off things till tomorrow, she thrived on crossing items off her to-do list. Otherwise, she wouldn't sleep peacefully at night.

As Strategy Director for City Investment Brokerage firm, she hadn't achieved her position by resting on her laurels. Sheer hard work and determination were traits she'd acquired early in life, and they drove her to the top of her career ladder.

Once the emails were sent, she stuffed her tablet into her oversized black leather Ferragamo handbag, picked up the vodka mixer drink Stella had left for her and relaxed into her overstuffed armchair.

"Sometimes, I wish I was as bold as Wumi so I wouldn't hesitate to go up to him." Releasing an appreciative sigh, Stella took another swig of her drink as if in consolation for her lack of bravery, or rather, coquettishness.

"On the other hand, I read somewhere that men like him prefer to do the hunting. Is that true?"

"Men like him?"

"You know, the Alpha type—dominant, assertive, confident men."

"Well, I wouldn't know." Faith rolled her eyes and glanced in the direction Stella had been staring as if drawn by a gravitational force. Of course, she didn't need to look. She knew exactly who her friend and colleague had been referring to.

Everybody knew who *he* was—Mark Essien, second son of Chief Essien, the Chairman of Apex Group of Companies. As CEO of Apex Investments, Mark had been named the second most eligible bachelor in Nigeria after his older brother, Felix.

She'd swatted up on information about him when she'd found out he was going to be their keynote speaker at this Finance conference in Johannesburg.

They'd been here all week but he'd only arrived on Friday. As he strode down the aisle of the conference centre to the platform to deliver his speech, she'd heard the soft gasp from Stella who'd been sitting next to her.

Faith had seen pictures of the tycoon in the press. But none of it had prepared her for seeing him in the flesh. And when his gaze had connected with hers while he'd been speaking, her breath had died in her throat for one long moment. She'd told herself her response had been from the brilliance of the sparkling stars in his dark eyes. Yet, the truth remained—he was the most intriguing and handsome man she'd ever come across.

His height alone should be intimidating against her five-feet-four-inches' petite stature. However, his head of thick, curly afro left longer than most executives of his business status indicated him as a man who made his own rules and didn't go by standards set by society. She didn't know what colour his eyes were, except that they were dark and compelling, balancing out the rather harsh and masculine facial features.

At this moment, he slouched against the bar, one lean, caramel-coloured hand resting on his thigh, the other holding a short glass with amber liquid that could've been whisky or brandy.

Boredom; his expression reeked of it, his sensuous lips curled in a non-smile as he paid no attention to the woman whose arm draped his shoulder in a possessive gesture— another friend and colleague of hers, Wumi Adekunle.

"From the looks of things, you're too late. Wumi has already claimed him," Faith said, although Mark didn't look like someone who could be claimed, if the little attention he paid their colleague proved anything to go by. "She wouldn't like you wading in on her territory."

"Damn!" Her friend's face fell in disappointment. "What I wouldn't give to bag one of the Essien brothers as a boyfriend. You know, I read they were worth billions of dollars."

"You don't need to bag an Essien to have a good life. You have a good job and you're earning good money." To prove her point, she did a rough estimate of Stella's outfit— the black, halter-neck, Donna Karan frilly dress and peep-toe stilettos cost enough to feed some families for a year in Nigeria. "Why do you need him or any man, for that matter?"

"*Ah, body no be wood o.*" Stella eyed her with one shaped brow raised. "I'm still a woman with needs, even if you choose not to be."

Faith ignored her snarky comment. For the past few years, she had been so focused on achieving her professional ambitions that she hadn't made time to get involved in a personal relationship.

Why did she have to apologise for the path she had chosen? Men were expected to focus on building a career and wealth. And yet, in this day and age, women were still expected to yearn for relationships and babies. No way. Not her.

"If you want sex, you can still get it without surrendering to a man like Mark Essien. I promise you, getting involved with him can only lead to trouble. You are better off finding someone else to fulfil your sexual needs."

"Perhaps. But he looks like a man who can fulfil a woman's sexual needs *and* more." Her friend tapped her lips with scarlet-tipped fingers as she gave Faith a quick, mock-disdainful once-over. "Are you seriously saying that if he asked you out, you would turn him down? Get real."

"No." Faith sucked in a sharp breath. "My answer to him would be 'no'."

She refused to give heed to the voice in her mind calling her a liar because she'd already imagined what it would be like to have Mark's intense gaze on her body. Even now, her body quickened at the thought.

"Sure even you as a Strategy Director of a brokerage firm can see the advantage of bedding one of the kings of finance. You're the career woman bent on getting to the top."

"But not like that!" She'd fought hard to attain her position in a male-dominated environment and didn't want any kind of speculation that she got there by sleeping around.

"I know. I was just joking." Stella patted her hand playfully. "But you've got to admit it's tempting, right." She wagged her eyebrows as she smiled. "I wonder, if you marry a king of finance, do you become a queen of finance?" she asked as if lost in thought.

The two of them looked at each other and burst out laughing. Several people turned around to stare at them. Faith couldn't stop the giggling until she felt eyes burning the back of her head and turned to find the very same man they were laughing about staring at her with his lips curled in amusement, too, for the first time that evening.

Instead of her laughter dying in her throat, butterflies fluttered low in her belly and her heart beat faster.

Wumi glared at her from where she stood next to Mark.

"Uh-oh!" Faith exclaimed and lifted her glass as she turned her back to hide her laughter.

"Oh, well, I'll have to go and introduce myself to him. I don't see why Wumi should be the only one enjoying his company," Stella remarked. She downed the rest of her drink in one huge gulp before heading back to the bar under the pretence of buying some more glasses.

Faith shook her head, not bothering to answer. If Stella thought she could muscle in on a man Wumi had already marked out for herself, she was in for a surprise.

They were all colleagues at City Investments—Faith the Strategy Director, Wumi the Deputy Finance Director, and Stella a Senior Financial Analyst. Three women who'd risen to the top and worked to support each other instead of backbiting like some other women did. They respected one another and watched each others' back in an industry that could be ruthless, sometimes.

Faith and Stella were originally booked to attend the annual conference in Jo'burg with the Finance Director, David Bode. But David had pulled out at the last minute, allowing Wumi to take his place.

Now, looking round the room, she could see quite a few of the guests from the conference looking the worse for wear. Today had been the last day of the event and usually, everyone let their hair down on the last night before they had to head back to different home destinations. There'd been people from all over Africa—Ghana, Kenya, Nigeria, and of course, South Africa.

The music, too, had grown louder. The deejay had changed the tracks from slow-jam R'n'B to up-tempo Afro beats. Watching the guests gyrating about the parquet dance floor, Faith felt old. She couldn't remember ever behaving so promiscuously, even when she'd been a teenager.

How sad was that? Her chest tightened, and her mouth dried out. Lifting her glass to her lips, she swigged her drink and allowed the buzz of the alcohol to kick in.

From the moment she left home to go to University, she'd had a five-year plan and nothing would derail it. Certainly not partying and men. She'd had a boyfriend at University but the truth was, Martin never held her heart. She'd never let her guard down long enough for any one man to mean anything to her. She liked it that way.

Moreover these days, as a director and member of the board, she couldn't party like some of the other people her age. For her, developing new strategies and thinking up ways to outdo their business rivals proved enough fun.

"Faith, look who I found." Stella returned, beaming from ear to ear. Behind her stood a tall, fit man in a navy, silk shirt and black trousers. "This is Marcus. You remember him?"

"Of course," Faith replied, smiling up at the South African man who'd been an attendee at the same seminars. "Good to see you again, Marcus."

"Same here, Faith." The man's lips curved in a charming smile as he held onto Stella's hand as if he didn't want to let go.

"We're going to have a dance. Want to come?" Her friend asked before leaning down to whisper in Faith's right ear. "He's gorgeous, isn't he?"

"He is," she replied in a low voice. Marcus had the whole 'Matthew Fox from Lost' thing going on, with close-cropped hair and shadowed chin. "Go and have fun. I'll catch you later."

Stella straightened, lines appearing on her usually flawless, pretty face. "I don't want you sitting all alone. Come with us."

"No. I'll be fine. You don't have to babysit me."

"Okay. I'll catch you later."

The two of them headed to the dance floor, Marcus still holding onto Stella's hand.

What does it feel like to have the undivided attention of a man who didn't want to let you go?

She'd never known that feeling. The tightness in her chest returned.

I need another drink if I'm suddenly longing for male company.

A glance at her glass revealed it empty. She should head to the bar and get it refilled. But there lay her problem. Mark Essien. Her head lightened at the thought of standing mere inches away from him.

"Men like him prefer to do the hunting." Her friend's words came back to haunt her. Her breath hitched and between her thighs throbbed a similar rhythm as her pounding heart.

Oh, God! Why did the idea of being hunted by Mark make her body come alive? Why did she suddenly crave his touch?

Snatching her tote, Faith left the lounge and hurried for the ladies'. She rubbed her wrist-watch in an agitated motion as she tried to quell her body's excitement. She avoided the bar area and manoeuvred through the exuberant crowd, smiling and giving quick greetings to some people she recognised from the seminars.

In the loo, the sound of music felt less intrusive, and she took the time to refresh her makeup and check her outfit. She'd changed from her skirt suit into a plum silk dress with a cowl neckline that hid her buxom bust line and skimmed her curves.

The overall impression of the outfit pointed towards sophisticated and understated sensuality, unlike Wumi's strapless, figure-hugging dress that obviously had men panting to gain her attention, including Mark Essien.

While Wumi had no problems flaunting her sexuality, Faith always struggled to ensure that people noticed her intelligence and her ability, not just that she had a body that could satisfy a man's needs or had childbearing hips.

A glance at her watch showed almost midnight. How much longer were her friends expecting to stay up at the party?

Faith massaged her temples, trying to push back the dull throbbing in her head, a sign of her tiredness. She'd been up since five a.m. that morning, trying to finish a presentation for investors which she would be delivering on Monday. She'd gone down to the hotel gym for a workout before showering and getting dressed for the day's events.

They'd had a full day of seminars culminating in the speech by Mark Essien on the future of African investments in a global market. She'd been really impressed with his conclusions, some of which she'd reached herself, especially since she'd been trying to convince her own board on some of the issues he'd highlighted.

After the seminar, she'd gone back to her room, showered, and changed before coming down to the dinner which had then transformed into a party. In the process, she'd called her parents to request that her brother come to Lagos to stay for a few weeks while on school break.

As usual, her suggestion had been shot down by her father. The man saw her as a corrupting influence on her young sibling. The anger of that disappointment had simmered all evening, partly the reason she hadn't gotten into a celebratory mood.

Now, all she wanted was her bed, before she had to wake up and catch a flight back to Lagos tomorrow.

Faith sighed again, opened the door, and stepped out of the ladies'.

She sucked in a startled breath at the sight of a man standing underneath the archway leading back to the dancehall.

Mark Essien.

His shoulder propped against the wall in a casual manner, his legs crossed over at the ankles, and his hand holding a smart phone which he shoved in his back pocket.

For a moment, she stood there and just stared at him, lean and unquestionably sexy, in grey pinstripe trousers and a black silk shirt, the sleeves rolled back over forearms liberally spread with fine, dark hair, two buttons undone at the collar so that she got a sneak peek of a muscular chest.

"Oh," she said, her voice a little squeaky as her mouth suddenly dried out. "Hi...Were you looking for the gents' toilet? I think it's on the other side of the hall."

She wasn't even sure why she was talking to him except that she suddenly couldn't control her mouth.

"No. I don't need the gents'," he said, his voice low and disturbingly sensual, spiking her nerves. "I was looking for you."

"Me?" Faith couldn't hide the surprise from her voice. What could he want with her?

"Yes...you," he agreed, with a smile that gave his words a disarming intimacy. "I think we should both get out of here. You don't want to be here any more than I do."

Faith blinked at the rate of a machine gun and turned away to gather her thoughts.

Wumi wouldn't be pleased if she could hear him. She'd spent the whole day talking about meeting up with him and then the entire evening following him around like a puppy.

"Admittedly—" She swallowed to clear her throat and tried again. "—I'm tired and was thinking of going up to my room. But we certainly don't have to leave together."

Winged creatures fluttered low in her belly as she struggled to believe he had come out here especially to see her. For heaven's sake, he didn't appear the kind of man who'd be interested in someone so ordinary. Attractive enough for a young woman, she didn't have Wumi's runway-model body, or Stella's pretty face.

Mark smiled—sensually curled lips, dimpled cheeks and eyes glinting with delightful mischief. Her insides melted. "There's nothing that says we can't."

Warmth radiated through her body and she couldn't help smiling even as she shook her head. "I think Wumi, your girlfriend—" She had to force the word out of her mouth. "—and my friend, will have something to say about that, don't you think?"

He rested his head against the frame of the door for a moment, studying her with eyes that she now saw were as dark as the midnight sky. Framed by thick, black lashes, they caused a shivery feeling inside her.

Just her luck. The first man she'd been attracted to in a very long time had to be involved with her friend.

He straightened and moved into the hallway.

Prey. She was being stalked. *Hunted.*

The rush of blood thundered in her ears, and her eyes widened, half in apprehension, half with a sense of anticipation she'd never felt before. *Pull yourself together, Faith.* There must have been way too much vodka in her mixer.

He tucked a stray strand of hair behind her ear, his fingertips brushing her earlobe. A shiver passed through her body and the subtle contraction in her lower belly returned.

Without going back to his original position, he said, "So, you must be Faith, right?"

Her gaze riveted to his lips quirked in amusement. Would they be soft or firm if she kissed him?

"Yes..." she replied in a breathless voice, her head inclined. "Faith Brown."

"I guess you know me already, but I'll introduce myself again. My name is Mark Essien," he said, with a slight bow of his head. "Nice to meet you."

"Oh, um, nice to meet you, too." Faith reared her head back in surprise when he held out his hand towards her. She was used to formal introductions at work. Still, something about Mark's intro told her this was personal, not business.

"The pleasure is mine," his voice dropped an octave and he took the hand she offered, raising it to his lips.

Faith imagined him brushing his lips against her knuckles. Mark surprised her by turning her hand over. Warm lips brushed her palm and for a second or two, his rough tongue flickered against her skin. Inside, she clenched low, needing to be filled. Outside, she tingled, craving more caresses.

Spellbound and unable to withdraw, she prayed he would release her so she could scrub her hand against her dress and pretend the kiss hadn't happened. She could pretend she wasn't being a bad friend and falling in lust with a man who was out of bounds to her.

There had to be a sisterhood rule about lusting after your friend's boyfriend, right?

God obviously didn't pay attention to her prayer because Mark didn't let her go. His eyes, cobalt and intense, studied her closely.

Spontaneous combustion in humans might be a scientific fiction. But, right here right now it might become her reality if she didn't detach from him.

"Mr. Essien—"

"Mark. You may call me Mark," he interrupted huskily, and her mouth went suddenly dry. "So long as you allow me to call you Faith. That is such a beautiful name."

A moan bubbled in her throat. Clamping her mouth shut, she suppressed it and took a shuddering breath.

Where did he learn such skills in seduction? According to the info she read about him, he'd be thirty-ish and at her last birthday she became twenty-eight years old. Yet, he had a way of making her feel inexperienced and out of her depths.

"You can call me what you like, er, Mark," she said and licked her lips, tasting her cherry lip gloss. "As long as you let go of my hand." She managed to pull her fingers free and forced a smile. "I gather you're not enjoying the party?"

He shrugged, broad shoulders moving sinuously beneath the expensive cloth of his shirt.

"Are you?" he countered, making no attempt to give her some space. He gestured about him. "Is that why you are hiding in here?"

Faith arched brows. "I'm not hiding," she replied and straightened her back.

All consuming eyes regarded her between narrowed lids. "We could hide together," he suggested, lifting a hand and tracing a long middle finger down the curve of her face from lip to jaw. "Would you like that?"

Skin tingling; she took an involuntary step backwards as her temper rose. "No. I wouldn't like that!"

How could she have allowed things to get this far? Whatever impression she'd given, she wasn't interested in a one-night stand. Not tonight. Not with him, anyway. Let Wumi satisfy his libido.

Unfortunately, he stood between her and the exit. She backed up, deciding to return into the ladies'. Perhaps he would just give up and leave her alone. For every step she took backward, he took one forward. She only managed to splay herself to the wall.

Now he stood before her, encroaching in her personal space. She reached forward to push him away but her fingertips encountered the taut muscles of his midriff. Heat rushed through her.

"I think you should go back to the party, Mr. Essien," she said, despite the fact that she'd called him Mark already. "I'm sure Wumi must be wondering where you are."

"I don't think so," he said, the deep quality of his voice feeling intimate.

"I don't want to upset Wumi," she said in a terse tone. Then, in an effort to lighten the conversation, she added, "You must be used to attending parties with different women."

That didn't come out the way she'd wanted it.

He didn't seem affected, though. His shoulders lifted in a shrug and he moved back to spread his arms on either side of her head.

"A hazard of my position. But I didn't come to this party with any woman. So I'm free to leave with whomever I choose," he remarked with dry humour. "So does that mean you've been reading up about me?"

Faith's lips parted, and for a moment, she forgot that she'd been trying to send him away. Eyes widening, she said in her defence, "Guilty as charged. But I can't really avoid it. News about you and your brothers are usually splashed on the tabloids and your business dealings on the business pages. It's unavoidable."

"True. If it makes you feel better, I looked you up as well before dinner."

Sucking in a sharp breath, she couldn't believe what she'd just heard. "Why?"

"I like to find out about anyone I'm going to get involved with, and I read loads of good things about you."

"Are you saying you want to get involved with me? How?" Her brain seemed to have stopped processing the words after 'get involved with.' "Is there a business project you want us to work on together?"

"Ah, no." His lips twisted in a mocking way. "Not a business project."

"Okay," she said, though, she thought it a pity. She could quite see the two of them collaborating on some venture. "So, what is it, then?"

"I want to get involved with you on a very personal level." His voice acquired a honeyed huskiness, flowing over her.

Her breath died in her throat for a few heartbeats as his words sank in.

His fiery gaze dropped down where the fabric draped over her breasts. Her nipples pebbled, grazing the lacy cup of her half-bra as he burnt a downward path on her body with his eyes. The way her body responded, he might as well be touching her already with those long fingers of his.

"What—what are you saying?" Faith spluttered in disbelief at her own reaction to his audacious words and actions.

His fingers brushed against her bare collarbone. Her pulse jumped beneath his touch.

"Don't do that! What if someone came in?"

Mark's mouth took on a sensual curve, but he obeyed, shifting his hands to the narrow bones of her shoulders.

"Is that the only reason you want me to stop, sweetheart?" he queried, those curious black eyes burning with a furnace fire.

She was actually trembling, and it infuriated her. For heaven's sake, what was wrong with her? She'd never felt quite so vulnerable in her life. Or so exhilarated.

"I think you should let go of me, Mr. Essien," she said in a stiff tone. "I'm afraid you've got the wrong impression."

"And if I don't want to?" he murmured, his thumbs probing inside the neckline of her dress.

"I don't think that matters," she retorted, refusing to let him see how he was affecting her. "I don't know what Wumi's told you about me, but I'm not interested in casual sex."

That shocked him, obvious in the sudden darkening of his eyes, the way the coppery stars dimmed to sombre cobalt. But he still didn't release her.

"Nor am I," he informed her. "And Wumi has told me nothing about you."

Faith's cheeks heated up. "I just meant—"

"I know what you meant, sweetheart." His sultry gaze impaled her. "Good girls don't put out so easily, right? I get it. We can talk, get to know each other a little first."

His fingers tightened a little and Faith caught her breath.

"No, I don't want to talk or do anything else you have up your sleeve," she replied, allowing her displeasure to seep into her voice. "Now, please...I'd like you to let me go."

"Did I offend you?" The scowl on his face only made him look adorable and she fought the urge to smooth out the lines on his face with her fingers. "I didn't mean to, if I did."

"No?" She knew exactly what he had intended. But right now, she'd grown more concerned with putting some breathing space between them. With his warm breath against her temple, and his fingers digging into her flesh, she struggled to keep her composure. She'd never been with a man who made her feel this vulnerable. "Well, whatever you meant, I'm not interested in massaging your ego."

"My ego?" He sounded amused. "So you think you know what kind of man I am?"

She shifted her weight from her right to left leg. "I think you're too sure of yourself probably because women always throw themselves at you."

White teeth showed between the sensual contours of his lips.

"You are so right, sweetheart. Some women do. But I prefer going after a woman I want. And I want you, Faith."

"No." Her eyes widened in horror and he gave a low laugh, disturbing the butterflies in her tummy.

"I do," he said in a smug tone, and, before she could respond, he bent his head and caught the corner of her lower lip between his teeth. He bit into the soft flesh.

A heavy dose of pleasure tinged with a little pain filled her. Her brain short-circuited, her protest disintegrating.

In a sensuous exploration, his mouth stroked across hers, for one long moment, as if preparing her for what came next. Without thinking, she opened, inviting him to probe further, wanting to feel him deep within, to taste all of him. He didn't hesitate, his tongue surged between her teeth. Flavours burst into her mouth, brandy and Mark, mixing to leave her intoxicated with him.

One firm hand circled her neck, his fingers tangling with the short strands of her hair. Silky locks tumbled over her ears and his knuckles, and his groan of satisfaction said it all.

A sound rose in her throat. Was it a cry to stop or a whimper of surrender? She didn't know anymore. This whole experience felt unreal. Things like this didn't happen to her. She never responded to men this way. One had actually called her frigid, but in Mark's arms, hot blood burned through her veins.

He moved so that she stood pressed back against the wall, the hard strength of his body moulded to hers. The kiss deepened and lengthened. His hands sought her hips, bringing her fully against him, so the evidence of his desire burnt her through the fabrics.

"What the hell do you think you're doing?"

Faith heard the angry exclamation as if from a distance. But its significance didn't register until sharp nails dug into her arm and tugged. Mark lifted his head, breaking the spell he had on her.

Wumi stood beside them, her face twisted with disapproval, one hand on her hip, the other still gripping Faith. Damning shame blazed across Faith's cheeks, replacing the utter euphoria singing in her veins.

"Wumi," she said, turning towards her. "I...it's not what you think."

"Isn't it?" Her friend didn't sound convinced.

Faith wasn't even sure. It had to be temporary insanity on her part. "I don't know what came over me," she admitted. "I must have had too much to drink."

"I know very well what would've come all over you if I hadn't found you. I thought we were friends, Faith."

"We are—"

"For goodness sake, aren't there enough men here for you to choose from without hitting on my man?"

"Wumi—"

Faith tried again, after a bare glance at Mark's scowling face. She couldn't make eye contact, didn't dare acknowledge what just happened between them.

Nevertheless, she registered his stillness, the fact that he'd pushed those long-fingered hands into the front pockets of his trousers. Her body still buzzed in remembrance of his caresses.

"Excuse me." Mark intervened. "I came to the party alone, Wumi. I may be many things, but I am not your man."

"Oh, please—"

"We were together earlier!" Wumi exclaimed, looking at Mark. "You wouldn't be here at all if I hadn't persuaded you to come to the party."

"I did not know your invitation came with strings attached," he retorted with ice dripping from his words. "You forget yourself. I do not need your permission to speak with Faith."

"To speak with her?" Wumi scoffed. "Is that what you call it? When I came in, you had your tongue halfway down her throat."

"And that concerns you how?" The tone of his voice thickened. "I suggest you leave us. We don't need you as a chaperone."

"Um...perhaps Mr. Essien should leave," Faith ventured, not looking at him as she spoke.

She heard his sudden intake of breath at her words.

"You don't mean it!" he said in a harsh voice.

But before she could respond, Wumi intervened.

"She does," she said, her smile triumphant. "Bye bye, Mark. I'll see you in Lagos."

Faith's gaze darted from Wumi's face to Mark's. What did that mean?

He strode towards the door, and for a moment, she thought he would leave without speaking again.

However, he halted on the threshold, gripping the wall door with one hand, the other scrubbing his scalp.

"This is not over, Faith," he said in a voice as soft as butter, and she didn't know whether that was a threat or a promise.

CHAPTER TWO

After Mark left, silence clanged in the air like thunder on a stormy night, loud and bloody uncomfortable.

"That was fun, wasn't it?" Wumi's words dripped with sarcasm.

Faith pressed her lips together. "Yes, well, I'd rather not talk about it, if you don't mind." She glanced down at her wristwatch, noticing the way her dress clung to her where Mark had been pressing against her, and cringed at the rumpled image she presented.

"Listen, I suggest you keep away from Mark Essien. He is not your type."

"How do you know my type?" Faith glared at Wumi. "Moreover, I'm not going to see him again."

"Good, because I wouldn't want to fall out with you because of him."

Wumi's snarky tone just grated on her nerves more.

"You know me well enough to know I have no interest in men," she retorted and shoved the ladies' door open. The panel banged against the wall with force.

"Mark is no ordinary man. He belongs in a different league and I had to persuade him to come to this party." Wumi followed her in and shut the door quietly behind her.

"Plus he is a man who always gets what he wants. Like a kid with a new toy when he meets a new woman, he's got to have her. And after he's played to his fill, he gets bored and moves on. I'm the only woman who has lasted in his life. We've been friends for years, and when it's time for him to settle down, I will be here for him."

Why did the idea of Mark settling with her friend stab her in the heart like a jagged knife?

"I have no intention of becoming Mark's toy. He will just have to go and play with someone else."

Faith smacked her palms against her dress, attempting to smooth out the rumple. Her thighs hurt from the impact and the pain grounded her, reminding her how foolish she'd been to allow a man like Mark to kiss her. Thankfully, she was in South Africa, and the only person who had witnessed the kiss was Wumi. "Look, please don't mention what happened with Mark to anyone."

"Of course, I'm not going to mention it to anyone. What do you take me for?"

"Thank you." She exhaled in relief. She didn't want her name entangled with Mark's as gossip fodder. "It's late. I think it's time we wrapped things up here. It's after one, and—"

"You're not serious?" Wumi's jaw dropped in disbelief. "Faith, you can't just go to bed. Things are just beginning to heat up. Just because you got a little tight and made a pass at Mark, I'm not going to hold it against you. We've been friends too long to let a man—"

Faith lifted a hand to silence her. "How do you know him, anyway? And what did you mean when you said you'd see him next week?"

"Oh." Wumi looked coy now. "Didn't he tell you? Well, I guess he didn't get a chance to explain. We are old family friends. The Essien brothers were in the same school as my brother."

"Oh." Faith nodded. "Oh, I see."

"I guess he must have been bored tonight because he doesn't usually hang out in places like this with the masses."

Faith was tempted to say there was nothing wrong with them, but she didn't want to give Wumi another excuse to patronise her. Moreover, Mark had indicated he wanted to leave the party, so her friend was probably right. At least about him not mixing with the common herd every day.

"Anyway, just because he's walked out doesn't mean we have to ruin the party," her friend continued when Faith didn't bite. "Another hour, Faith. Pretty please? Then we can all get to bed, I promise."

Mark walked back to his suite in the hotel. The relative quiet should have offered him peace, yet his mind remained plagued with thoughts of Faith.

He'd been so angry when she'd asked him to leave that he hadn't thought about anything but getting out of there. Women didn't normally dismiss him so readily. In fact, he couldn't remember anyone who had said no to his advances. Certainly not after returning his kiss with as much passion as Faith had done.

The tingle on the back of his neck returned as he recalled when he'd first seen her sitting in the front row of the seminar hall. She had this whole Halle-Berry-short-hair-cut going on that accentuated her pretty narrow face and fitted in with a conservative grey skirt suit with black edges.

When she smiled, seemingly at something he'd said, her sensuous lips curled at the edge and her eyes—beautiful, intelligent eyes—flared with a luminous quality. His breath had caught and he'd lost his train of thought. He'd had to glance at his notes to continue his speech. The first time ever since he had to present his thesis as an undergraduate. All his presentations were delivered from memory alone and he never referred to his notes. Until today.

He stripped off his clothes and headed for the shower. The cascade of jets of water on his skin always soothed him. But as he massaged shower gel onto his skin, an image of Faith popped back into his head. Standing close to her in that alcove had confirmed his suspicions. Her earlier business suit hid a voluptuous figure. Her brows were several shades darker than her honey-streaked cropped hair.

What would she look like with no clothes on? What would she feel like? The base of his spine tingled and his arousal flared. He groaned out loud. If Wumi hadn't interrupted them, he could have had Faith up in his room right now. She could've been right here in the shower with him, crushed against the tiles while he touched and tasted her.

His lips twisted. When Wumi had invited him to the party, he'd intended to decline. He wasn't in the habit of mixing business with pleasure. But she'd been so insistent, and he'd wanted an opportunity to meet with Faith after seeing her at the seminar.

Frustrated, he shut off the faucet and snatched a towel as he stepped back into the bedroom, patting his body dry. He chucked the towel and pulled on a pair of boxer briefs and groaned as the stretchy material tugged at his hard-on.

Why the hell was he torturing himself over one woman? There were plenty of them who would've been happy to take Faith's place. He could get dressed and head back to the bar downstairs. He would definitely get laid tonight.

Or he could simply make a phone call. Wumi had been hinting that she would be more than willing to warm his bed that night. All he had to do was pick up the phone and dial her number and she'd be up here.

He shook his head and pulled back the sliding door to the balcony of his suite. The Johannesburg city skyline beckoned, lit in gold and blue against a cobalt sky.

Bedding Wumi presented a lot more hassle than she'd be worth. For starters, any involvement with Wumi came with strings attached. She was a family friend. If his parents so much as got a whiff that they were involved, his mother would be planning the wedding already.

And Wumi wasn't the only woman who wanted to get her manicured fingers on an Essien. If they lined up, they would be queuing around the block where the luxury hotel was situated. And they were all interested in the same things. Wealth. Power. Influence. Being married to an Essien provided these privileges.

He should know. His mother had been one of those women for whom these things had been important. Otherwise, why else would she have gotten involved with his father when the man had been married and out of bounds?

Stepping out, he shivered more from dread than from the cold. Wedding bells and commitment were definitely not on his agenda tonight or any other night. Yes, he loved female company. But he certainly couldn't trust any of them. Sex. Mutual pleasure. Even friendship, of sorts, proved okay.

Experience had proven women couldn't be trusted. His brother, Felix, recently had to sue a national Newspaper for a libellous publication where they'd printed that he'd fathered a son and abandoned the boy and mother. Though Felix had since forgiven the woman who had made the false claim because she had desperately needed funds to care for her sick boy, Mark did not forgive the woman so readily. It only strengthened his case against their gender.

With a sigh, he leaned against the concrete railing. One look down at his underwear confirmed his erection had diminished. One good thing thinking about women and weddings bells did for him.

Although, one woman still plagued his mind. One with soft curves he could lose himself in and a mouth designed to provoke a man's desire.

Faith. She'd certainly been different from the other girls at the party. Her almost shy manner was a rarity to see in women these days, especially for someone with a professional track record like hers.

Had she been playing hard to get? He'd learned early that some women enjoyed the games, feigning disinterest just to have a man fawn over them.

Somehow, he hadn't sensed the same vibe from Faith. She had felt so good in his arms. Warm, soft, and sexy. Her résumé claimed she was close to twenty-eight but she looked younger. She seemed so innocent, somehow. He wanted to see her again. But would she want to see him? He would find out her room in the morning and arrange a date with her for when they got back to Lagos.

Happy with his resolution, he shut the balcony door and headed for bed. Sleep came swiftly due to his long day. He dreamt of a certain woman with cropped hair and chocolate eyes.

In the morning, he put his charm to good use as he wrangled Faith's room number out of the receptionist...only to find out she had already checked out, presumably to catch a morning flight back to Lagos.

Disappointed, he didn't allow the news to derail his plans. After breakfast, he packed, ready for his flight to Lagos in the afternoon.

Once in Lagos, his busy schedule meant he didn't get the opportunity to contact her until halfway through the next week when his assistant got him her work address and phone number. He called when he had a break at lunch.

"City Investments, how can I help you?" a soft-spoken woman who wasn't Faith answered the call.

"I'd like to speak to Faith Brown, please."

"Ms. Brown is not available at the moment. But I'm Amara, her assistant. I can take a message for her."

He bit down the disappointment and carried on. "Is she in the office or out?"

"May I know who's asking, sir?"

Mark smiled at the savvy question. Faith had obviously acquired a smart assistant.

"This is Mark Essien."

There was a pause on the line.

"As in Mr. Mark Essien from Apex Investments?" She sounded a bit doubtful.

"Yes, that very same Mr. Mark Essien," he said, not hiding his amusement.

"Oh...sorry, sir. I will let Faith—Ms. Brown know that you called. Was there anything specific you wanted me to tell her?"

"No need to apologise. Just tell her to call me back when she becomes available."

"I will, sir. Have a nice day."

"And you, too, Amara."

He hung up and returned to work expecting her call.

But she didn't call him back that day, or any other day, for that matter. Admittedly, his ego was stung. But he wasn't known for giving up easily. He just had to think of some way of finally getting together with the elusive Faith Brown.

Faith had gotten his message from a star-struck Amara when she'd exited her meeting later that afternoon. She didn't begrudge the dreamy expression in her assistant's eyes as the girl explained that Mr. Mark Essien had called asking for her. In the African money markets and Finance world, he proved something of a celebrity.

So to speak to him on the phone felt akin to speaking to Michael Jackson on the line. All the men aspired to be him, and all the women dreamed of marrying him. Amara walked around in a daze that afternoon with stars in her eyes. Faith had to tell her off when she brought the wrong client portfolio to her for a meeting she had the next day.

All that emphasised the reason Faith wouldn't talk to Mark again. She certainly didn't want to become one of the many thousands of women drooling after him in public. Although she couldn't discount the fact that after their encounter in Jo'burg, she'd been dreaming about him almost every night.

So no, she wasn't calling him, didn't want to listen to that deep, sensuous voice, as it did unthinkable things to her insides. She focused on work and pushed thoughts of Mark to the back of her head.

Faith kicked her high heels off her achy feet as soon as she walked into her townhouse in Lekki later that evening. She slumped on the sofa and massaged her temples. She had only two things on her mind—shower, and bed.

Her phone rang as she dumped her bag on the coffee table. She dug it out.

"Ebony!" she exclaimed as she answered the phone.

"Ha, Faith. You just abandoned me in this your Lagos," her friend replied in mock anger.

"*Abeg*. No vex. It's just been non-stop for the past few weeks and with the conference in Jo'burg last week, I only got back on Saturday and I've been preparing for a major meeting with investors this week. I should've called you."

"You should've. I'm going stir-crazy since my arrival with all the visitors milling around my parents' house and all the preparations for Chidi and Dad's memorial."

"Oh, I forgot all about that. How are you coping?"

"My dear, it's tough. I keep a brave face when people are around, but in the quiet of my room, the memories keep rushing back and replaying themselves."

"Oh, sweetie. Don't go upsetting yourself again. It will get easier. I think once the ten-year memorial is done with, you'll feel a lot better. I think it's harder because you haven't been back to Nigeria since they were buried. It must be a shock coming back and seeing where it all happened."

"You don't know how much of a shock it is. But now it's compounded because of this shenanigan with Dele."

"You know that Dele man deserves a hit squad for what he did to you. After all you did for him, he had the guts to du—cancel your wedding just weeks before it's due. Can you imagine the nonsense?"

"I know. Ten years of my life wasted on a man who wasn't even worth it."

"Dele is heartless. He deserves to burn in hell. It's men like him that prove my case when I say I don't want to get involved with one of their kind."

"You can be sure I'm not in a rush to get involved with another man. Talking about men, did I tell you who picked me up at the airport when I arrived?"

"No, you didn't. Who?"

"Felix Essien. You know, the kings of Finance Essien brothers."

"No way!"

"Yes, way! Definitely him. And those magazine pictures do him little justice. That. Man. Is. A. God. On. Legs. I had to practically scrape my mouth off the floor."

Faith laughed. "You're kidding me."

"I kid you not. It turned out my mum had arranged with his dad for him to come to the airport and pick me up."

Faith laughed even harder. "Mumsie is matchmaking o. But by the way, how do you guys know the Essiens?"

"We're supposed to be long-time family friends. Apparently, his mum and my mum where in school together. Go figure that one."

"Wow. Isn't that a coincidence? I met Mark Essien last week at the conference. He was a speaker in one of the seminars." She avoided telling her friend that he'd kissed her since it wouldn't be happening again. Moreover, she wanted to focus on Ebony. "So, tell me about Felix, then. What was he like?"

"Actually, very charming and kind. I got a bit annoyed because I'd been expecting Afam, our family driver, so I got snarky with him. But he took it all in his stride and somehow, I found myself talking to him about Chidi and Dad. Turns out he remembers Chidi. They used to hang out together as kids."

That's something Felix had in common with his brother, Mark—the ability to make women talk without much prompting.

"Nice. So I predict romance in your future," Faith joked.

"Me and Felix? You've got to be kidding. Didn't you hear me say that I'm not interested in men? I still haven't gotten over Dele and you want me to get involved with someone else. I don't think so."

"But you're the one who said Felix was charming."

For as long as Faith could remember, Ebony had been in a relationship. She'd fallen in love as a teenager and stayed faithful to the same man for over ten years.

"Yes, he is." Her friend sounded excited. "But I'm not ready. And he doesn't seem to be interested, anyway. He hasn't been in touch since the day he dropped me off at the house in Ikoyi."

"You never know." She understood her friend as one of those people who thrived in the stability of a steady commitment. Being unattached added to Ebony's listlessness and Faith hoped the man who would love and appreciate her would come along soon. If that proved to be Felix Essien, so be it. "Anyway, what are you doing on Friday?"

"Me?" Ebony replied. "Nothing *o*. What do you have in mind?"

"How about we go out? There's this nice new bar and restaurant in Victoria Island I'd like to check out." She tucked her phone between her ear and shoulder and walked to her bedroom with her bag dangling from her arm.

"I'd love to. What time do you want to meet?"

Bag on bed, Faith pulled out her tablet and scrolled through her calendar. "Is seven o'clock right for you?"

"Works for me," her friend answered.

"Great. I'll pick you up." She made a note on her virtual schedule and set a reminder. Otherwise, she'd forget. "Give my love to mumsie. Tell her I'm coming soon to eat *Ofe Onugbu*."

In her late teen years, Ebony's mother acted as Faith's foster mum and they still had a great relationship.

"I will." Ebony's soft laughter filtered through the phone. "Silly me, I didn't ask about your mum. How is she doing?"

"She is doing okay. Going on about the usual things— me getting married and having babies. As if." Faith hissed. She loved her mother. But sometimes the woman drove her nuts.

"I've told you to take it easy on your mum. She only wants what every other parent like her wants."

"What's that?"

"Grandchildren, of course." Ebony laughed.

"Grandchildren, my foot. In short, get off my phone now," Faith said in mock annoyance, while smiling.

"I'll see you on Friday," Ebony carried on laughing before hanging up.

Faith put her phone on her bed and went into the bathroom to shower. But Ebony's words stayed in her mind. Later while she slept, she dreamed about her mother and little babies crawling around the house. In the middle of the night, she jolted awake covered in cold sweat.

After the busy week, Faith was in a great mood when Friday night came along and she drove over to Ebony's house to pick her up. She had the radio on in the car, listening to the DJ and his 'American' accent. She even sang along to Rihanna's "Shut Up and Drive."

Looking forward to seeing her childhood best friend after they hadn't seen each other for over five years had her practically skipping to the door after she parked her car in their driveway and the housekeeper let her in.

Having lived in this house awhile ago, she didn't need a guide to find her way around. As expected at this time of day, she found Mrs. Duru in the main lounge.

"Good evening, Mummy."

She'd started addressing the woman that way since their secondary school days when Ebony's mother used to visit them on visiting days and bring loads of food and snacks for both Ebony and Faith.

Mrs. Duru had always treated her as if she was her own child. The woman seemed to know instinctively about the problems Faith had been having with her own family and adopted her in. There had been occasions when her own mother hadn't come to see her in school. But Ebony's mother had been there and Faith had felt as if someone had cared about her during those moments.

"Good evening, my dear. How are you doing?" Mrs. Duru replied as Faith leaned over to hug her in the armchair.

"I'm doing very well, thanks."

"How are your parents and sibling doing? Do you get to see them often?"

"Yes, I was in Benin a few months ago. But I speak to my mum regularly. Everyone is doing fine," she said as she took as seat on one of the upholstered sofas.

"That's good. Should I ask Margaret to bring you a drink or something to eat while you wait for Ebony?"

"Ah, Mummy, don't worry. If I want something, I'll go and get it myself. I'm not a visitor," she joked.

"Of course you're not. You're my second daughter. How's work going? Ebony was telling me that you've been promoted to Strategy Director. Congratulations. You work so hard and you deserve it."

"Thank you, Mum. I'm really excited about my new role but I love it. Although it means more work and responsibilities."

"Oh, I'm sure you're equal to the task. All you need now is a nice young man to make you happy. I'm sure your parents would like to have their first grandchild soon."

Grandchildren again! Was this some kind of cosmic conspiracy or something?

Faith bit her tongue instead of replying, so that she didn't say something rude to the woman she respected like a mother. Why did people seem to think a woman wasn't complete unless she became a baby factory for some man who wouldn't even appreciate her?

No, thank you!

"How are the preparations going?" She changed the subject.

"They're going well," Mrs. Duru said. "It's a big shame it isn't going to be the double celebration we hoped for."

Faith nodded, sadness making her heart ache. Ebony's wedding to Dele had been planned to take place in Lagos a month after the memorial ceremony. The preparations had already been made and invitation cards sent out. But Dele had only phoned Ebony to call the whole thing off a few days before she was due to arrive in Nigeria. The coward of a man couldn't even wait to speak to her face to face, his excuse being that the earlier they called it off, the less of an inconvenience it would become for their guests.

Bastard!

"Anyway, I'm glad you're taking her out tonight," Mrs. Duru continued. "She's been almost depressed since her arrival home and moping around. Hopefully, she'll get to relax and have fun tonight so she can realise that there is life after Dele."

Double bastard!

Faith hated how a man upset Ebony, so much so, her mother had noticed it. She really could wring Dele's neck.

Another good reason she should avoid men. She never wanted to be left that vulnerable and devastated. It took her a long time to work her confidence and self-esteem to a point where she became comfortable in her own skin after all that problems she'd had at home growing up. She certainly didn't want to allow a man to destroy everything she'd single-mindedly built for herself.

Ebony arrived dressed up in a red silk cocktail dress with spaghetti straps, low neckline, and frilly skirt that stopped just above her knees and showing off long smooth legs, her feet in strappy red stilettos.

"You look lovely, dear," her mother said.

"Yeah, you'll knock them dead tonight," Faith said as she hugged her friend.

"Thank you," Ebony replied, grinning from ear to ear. "I'm ready."

They bid goodbye to Mrs. Duru and left. Faith drove them to the bar which wasn't very far from Ebony's house. Judging by the busy state of the car park, the venue would be jam-packed. She managed to slip into a parking space when someone vacated it.

"Do you want to eat or just have some light refreshments?" she asked as they got out of the car.

"I'm not really hungry, so light refreshments would be fine."

"Okay. We'll head over to the bar lounge, then."

They walked into the dimly lit bar section of Reams. Afro beats thumped through hidden speakers. People lounged on dark brown leather sofas, conversations mingling with laughter and music. Most of the crowd of young professionals there at this time of the evening had come from work and were just allowing the Island traffic to reduce before they headed home.

She searched for a vacant booth they could sit in. From the corner of her eye, she spotted Mark Essien and her heart stopped.

He's here!

He hadn't seen her yet, and she should've looked away and dragged Ebony out of there. But she couldn't look away.

Then he peered up and their eyes connected and he smiled—that charming, knock-your-pants-off smile that always melted a bit of her insides.

Her heart pounded in her chest, her cheeks heating up as she remembered how he'd kissed her with those lips of his.

"I found an empty table." Ebony tugged her arm, oblivious to the turmoil unfolding inside her.

Faith followed her, glad for the distraction to snap away from Mark's heated gaze. But it seemed she wasn't going to be let off the hook that easily. As soon as they'd made themselves comfortable in the seats and were looking over the aperitif menu, Felix stood in front of them.

"Hello, Ebony," he said.

Ebony glanced up and Faith saw the way her eyes widened with surprise and her lips curled in a smile. It seemed her friend was really pleased to see Felix, which didn't quite match Faith's response at seeing Mark again.

"Hi, Felix."

The way Ebony replied, Faith knew her friend was a goner.

He leaned in to give her a peck on the cheeks as they exchanged pleasantries.

Faith used to the opportunity to glance over to where Mark sat. He was still looking at her, causing her heart rate to double its speed, his expression amused and collected.

Faith turned back to Ebony and tugged her arm as it seemed her friend had been so wrapped up in Felix, she'd forgotten about her.

"Felix...this is my friend, Faith."

"Hi, Faith. It's nice to meet you." Felix flashed a smile as charming as his brother's.

"Likewise," she replied, stretching out her hand to shake his, which he shook briefly before turning back to face Ebony. Obvious how keen he was on her friend.

"I'm here with my brother. Would you like to join us?" He nodded in the direction he'd come from.

Ebony stared enquiringly at her and Faith gave her a knowing look and shrugged. They were already here and it seemed they couldn't avoid the men now. Ebony seemed keen to chat with Felix and Faith didn't want to be the spoilsport. After all, they were supposed to be letting their hair down and, as they say, 'the devil you know is better than the angel you don't'. These two Essiens were as tempting as the devil himself.

"Sure. Why not? The more the merrier, right?" Ebony said.

Felix led them back towards the bank of sofas. Mark stood as they approached. He was as tall, dark, and devilishly handsome as he'd been the night they'd met. Tonight, he looked exceptional in his baby blue silk shirt and navy pinstripe trousers. His shirt had the top two buttons undone, showing off the dark V of his neck and chest. The sleeves of his shirt had been rolled up, revealing well-toned lower arms dusted with short dark hairs. His wide smile softened the harsh angles of his combatant face and his midnight eyes sparkled.

This close together, she could see he presented the spitting image of Felix, except for maybe their skin tones, Felix's being darker. No mistaking the fact they were brothers.

"Mark. Fancy meeting you here," she said, her voice louder than she wanted it to be.

"Faith. It's nice to see you again."

Mark had a lazy smile on his face as he kissed her on both cheeks. She caught a whiff of his spicy aftershave, reminding her of the night in Jo'burg. He'd had the same scent, woodsy and arousing. Now, her body quickened again, heat unfurling in her belly.

Strange, when he stepped back, she experienced a sense of loss. Her body liked the strength and closeness of his. They held each other's gaze for a moment and nothing else mattered.

"You two know each other?" Felix asked with a mix of surprise and humour, his dark brow arching upwards.

"You could say that. We met at a Finance conference in South Africa. And this must be Ebony," Mark said, smoothly turning to Ebony. "It's great to finally meet you. I've heard so much about you." He winked mischievously at Felix who, in turn, glared at him furiously.

"Really?" Ebony asked with amusement.

Faith observed the brothers. Their interaction reminded her of the kind of relationship she'd developed with Ebony, more her sibling than her own blood relatives.

"Mark, I warn you. I'll wring your neck if you say another word." Felix glowered and his brother simply laughed in response, the sound filled with warmth and delight.

"Don't mind Mark. He's just playing the fool. Please sit down," he said to Ebony before turning another withering look onto Mark who kept chuckling, although his gaze remained fixated on Faith.

The men waited for the ladies to sit down; Mark sat next to Faith and Felix next to Ebony. Faith exchanged amused looks with Ebony at the cosy set up.

"Why didn't you return my call?" Mark asked after the waiter had taken their drinks orders.

"I've had a very busy week at work," she said, lifting her shoulder in a blasé shrug, an attempt to mask the more than casual sensations twirling in her belly.

"Is that the real reason, or are you avoiding me?"

She glanced at him and lowered her gaze to the table, not wanting him to see how much he affected her.

"I'm not avoiding you, although I think we don't really have anything more to say to each other."

His hand settled on her left thigh, branding her with strength and heat, her fitted linen pencil skirt providing little protection for her awakening skin.

"There's still plenty we haven't said to each other. So much about you that I want to find out."

"Why?" A part of her still couldn't believe a man like him would be interested in her.

"You fascinate me. You're such a ball of contradictions. As a business professional, I know you're capable, bold, and ambitious. But last week, I saw uncertainty and vulnerability within you, standing in that alcove, and it makes me want to take you into my arms and protect you."

"O-kay." A flush crept across her face and she looked away. "You're very direct, aren't you?"

The waiter returned with their drinks and left.

"I believe in calling things as I see them. There's no point in playing games," Mark said.

Faith took a gulp of her vodka and coke to shore up her courage. "Well, since you're being direct, I guess I have to let you know that there can never be anything between us."

"Oh?" Dark eyes scanned her body in a slow appraisal. Her cheeks heated up. "I like you and it seemed obvious to me last week on Friday that you like me, too, by the way you responded to my kiss before Wumi interrupted us. So, what's the problem?"

Lowering her lashes coyly, she glanced at him through their dark veil and noticed him watching her without flinching. Their gazes connected, his black eyes now with flecks of crimson turning her already heated blood into lava. For a moment, she forgot what she was about to say.

She pulled her gaze away and concentrated on her words. "For starters, Wumi is my friend and it looks like she wants you for herself."

"Let me make this clear, in case you didn't understand me last week." He took her hand and held it between both his surprisingly soft palms, his expression serious. "I have no personal interest in Wumi. She is the sister of a friend. In fact, her brother was in school with Felix and me; that's how we know each other. We have never been romantically involved and never will be, no matter how much she wants it. Do you understand?"

She nodded, partially relieved he wasn't entangled with Wumi. But still, she couldn't get involved with him. She screwed her face into a frown.

"Was that the only reason you didn't want to see me?"

She stared at Ebony and Felix who seemed too engrossed in each other as they danced on the floor to even notice what went on with her and Mark. She hadn't even seen them stand to go to the dance floor.

"Look, Mark, you are an Essien. There are loads of women out there who clamour for your attention. I'm just not one of them. And I'm not in the dating market."

His head flinched back and his eyes narrowed in a confused expression.

CHAPTER THREE

With grace, Mark uncoiled his body from the sofa, rising to his impressive six-foot height, making Faith's heart thump against her chest as his arm extended in her direction and his sexy drawl reached her ears.

"Let's get out of here."

Her turn to be surprised. "What about Ebony and Felix?"

"I think those two don't need us cramping their style."

Faith nodded and smiled when she saw the way Felix held Ebony on the dance floor. She took Mark's hand and allowed him to pull her up. "Where are we going?"

"I know this nice place that does the best *Suyas* ever. I hope you like spicy grilled meat," he said as he ushered her towards the doors, his hand on the small of her back in a possessive gesture.

"I love *Suya*, although I try not to eat too much of it."

"I didn't bring my car so we'll take Felix's car. His driver can drop us off."

"No, I've got mine. I can drive." She took her keys out of her bag and pointed at the Infiniti FX, pressing the remote lock. The lights flashed and the car beeped.

"Nice," Mark said as he got into the passenger seat after she slid into the driver side.

"Thank you." She'd ordered the car when the company confirmed her promotion to director position. A big treat buying a new car, but the old one she'd been driving had become unreliable with needing one thing or the other repaired almost every month. She'd decided to grit her teeth and get a new vehicle.

A first, having a man in her car. Apart from the odd times when she had her kid brother in here with her, even her father had never been in it.

Mark directed her but she'd already guessed it would be the place on Ahmadu Bello Way. She headed in that direction, past the skyscrapers of international hotels and businesses, expensive shopping malls, and posh restaurants. Steam billowed out of vents in walls, mixing with exhaust fumes.

At that time of the evening, the night lit up in gold and blue glows of street lamps as well as red and white flashes of car taillights and headlamps. People milled around, either arriving at their destination or heading home. The sound of car horns and street vendors provided an almost melodic soundtrack to the feverish vibe. She loved the hectic atmosphere of living in the vibrant city of Lagos. In fact, she flourished in it.

A long column of cars met them when they arrived at the popular *Suya* spot.

"That's quite a queue," she commented.

"Yeah, kinda reminds me of the line to buy crepes in a popular spot up in Hampstead, London."

"Oh my God! I know the place; just on the High Street. I spent two weeks last year in London and my friend insisted we go to the *Crêperie*. How do you know it?"

"My family has a holiday home off Hampstead Heath. Outside of Lagos, the area is like a second home, really."

"Wow." Another reminder their backgrounds were so different. Her father couldn't afford to buy one, let alone own, a second property in an expensive area of a foreign country.

"I'll get off here and walk the rest of the way," Mark said as he undid his seatbelt. "Was there anything special you wanted on yours?"

"No. Just beef *Suya*. Actually, skip the onions on mine, thanks."

He smiled and got out. She watched him stride towards the outdoor restaurant, his swagger oh-so-sexy. She couldn't keep her eyes off him until he disappeared behind a car.

What was she doing with him? This all seemed so innocent, coming out to buy *suya* with him. Yet, it also proved intimate. She couldn't remember the last time she'd done anything close to this with a man. Mark grew more irresistible the more time she spent with him.

She'd only wanted to spend time catching up on old times with her friend— *Oh no! Ebony!*

She dug her phone out of her bag and sent her a text, telling her where she and Mark had gone. The line moved up and she drove closer to where Mark stood waiting for his order. Soon, he'd returned in the car with the two takeaway parcels.

The spicy scent of roasted meat filled the interior and her stomach chose that moment to rumble.

"That smells so good. It's been a long time since I ate this," she said as she laughed. "Do you want us to go back to Reams?"

"It's been years since I ate it, too," he said. "No. I would've said, let's go to my apartment which isn't far from here, but I already know what your response will be to that. So instead, head towards Kuramo Beach. There's a spot where we can sit out and eat and chat in seclusion."

"I didn't figure you for the kind of person to eat food out of a paper bag," she said as she drove off again, giving him a side glance.

His resonant, warm laughter filled the car. "You mean on account of the silver spoon one's got in one's mouth," he said in a very upper-class British accent.

She burst out laughing.

"As a king of finance," he continued in the same voice, his eyes twinkling with amusement, "one must interact with one's subjects once in a while, don't you think?"

"Of course," she replied, trying not to giggle so much at his impression of English nobility from the middle ages.

"And you must address me as 'Your Majesty'." He raised his nose. "I am a king, after all."

"Oh my gosh! I think you would make a very good comedian. You know what, I think you would give AY and Basketmouth a run for their money."

She stopped her car on the sands close to the beach.

"Oh, madam. But I only ever entertain select guests. I'm afraid the masses will be unable to afford my fees."

She knew he was joking but somehow, his words made her feel special, as if he really only did his comic act for her.

As if he sensed her thoughts, his laughter died away just as hers did. He captured her gaze once more and held her in his stare, her breath caught in her throat.

Would she ever get used to the intensity of his blue-black eyes or the fire that burned in their depth when he looked at her like that? It suddenly seemed as if his face was closer. Did she move towards him or was he the one that moved? She wasn't sure. All she knew was that their lips were going to touch if one of them didn't pull back.

She should stop this now. This was madness. She still hadn't recovered from his kiss a week ago. If he kissed her again, she would be lost.

But she couldn't move away from him to save her life. Instead, the magnetic pull dragged her closer.

Beep!

The blare of a car horn roused her and she leaned back into her seat, breathing a sigh of relief. That had been close.

"Just drive down a little further," he said in a suddenly husky voice.

Perhaps he had been as affected by their closeness as she'd been.

Faith followed the queue of cars until she found a space to park on the beach. As a location used for concerts and other entertainment events, finding a spot would've been difficult.

Not this evening. Miles of uncluttered white sand and gentle crashing blue waves greeted their arrival. Copper and red flickered in the distance, flames from a bonfire licking the briny air.

Mark stepped out, taking the food parcels with him. She opened her car door and lowered her feet. Her shoes sank into the powdery ground, grainy sand scouring her skin beneath the straps of her Jimmy Choo stilettos. Not the correct footwear for the landscape. Her lips curled down in an arch.

"What's wrong?" Concern tinged the low tone of Mark's query.

"I'm going to have to change my shoes." She reached back into her bag and withdrew the pair of coral lace ballerina flats. They lived in her bag and came in handy in her office when she needed to relax and give her feet a rest from the killer heels.

"Sit."

She arched her brow in response to Mark's order. "Excuse me?"

One—taking orders had never been her strong point. Two—when she did, it would be in a business environment from her boss.

These days, she only answered to one boss, the owner of City Investments. Taking orders from men-friends? Hell, no!

Moreover, had he changed his mind about the beach?

He met her no-nonsense glare, his dark eyes concentrated on her, the right corner of his lips curled up in what seemed to be a slow-building smile. She'd seen that grin before. The night they'd met for the first time in Johannesburg. The night he'd kissed her and become the subject of her night dreams, to her great chagrin.

"Let me help you take your shoes off." He sounded unfazed by her glower.

"Oh." Swallowing her embarrassment, she lowered her bum back onto the leather car seat, sitting sideways. She needed to learn to relax around men. But she hadn't dated in years. Although this wasn't a date.

He squatted beside the car. Cool, firm fingers wrapped around her left ankle. However, a white-hot zap travelled from her leg to between her thighs. Biting her lower lip, she suppressed a moan, her body's response to him catching her off guard.

It didn't help that whatever position he occupied, he still oozed sexy charm. Now, with his attention focused on her feet as he undid the straps, tugged off the stilettos, and slipped on the flats, his fingers feathered her skin in sensual caresses. Blood rushed in her ears, mixing with the sound of her thumping heart.

How can something as mundane as changing shoes be so erotic? Her fingers curled into the edge of the seat as she fought the urge to reach out the tangle them in his kinky hair.

Unable to resist the impulse, she scanned his body—the bunch of muscles under his forearms as he tugged and pulled the footwear, the expanse of broad shoulders, the hint of dark hair and caramel skin in the V of his open shirt, the stretch of fabric on his muscular thighs where they bunched from his crouch.

What was it Stella had said about Mark that night in Johannesburg? *He looks like a man who can fulfil a woman's sexual needs, and more.*

Right now, she could settle for the sexual needs part. She didn't need more.

Mark straightened. His palms burnt a path of electric energy on either side of her quivering, traitorous body and settled on her ribs as he lifted her out of the car until she stood on the sand.

This time, she didn't sink. She could've been floating for all she noticed, her gaze locked onto Mark's intensity.

He's going to kiss me and I seem incapable of stopping him.

Her breath locked in her throat, desire rooting her to the spot, liquefying her limbs.

"*Oga*, I have chairs for you over here."

Mark turned his head, breaking the spell. "Where is it?" he asked the beach boy who'd approached them.

The boy pointed to a row of white plastic chairs and tables covered in colourful umbrellas.

Faith drew in a long breath in relief. Saved by the interruption. With the reprieve, she tossed her stilettos into the back on the car and patted down her shift linen dress, getting her composure back.

With a smile on his face, Mark held out his hand. She stared at the long fingers extended in invitation and tried not to think about the devastation they'd just caused to her body.

I can do this. Mark is just a friend. This is just friends hanging out. No more. No less.

With a puff of breath to bolster her resolve, she placed her hand in his. They walked across the shifting sands and she ignored the tingles travelling down her arms.

He helped her into her seat, deposited the food and drinks on the table, and tipped the boy.

"*Oga*, thank you," he said and moved on when he saw some more people coming to the beach.

With Mark seated, their gazes met again and she lowered her eyes, not wanting to get lost in his dark pair again. That's when she noticed she subconsciously rubbed her left palm which Mark had been holding, as if clinging on to his lingering warmth.

I'm in so much trouble.

The corner where they sat didn't have direct light, lit only by the silver streaks of the rising moon. Mark handed her one of the parcels. She unwrapped it, revealing a stack of sliced grilled beef kebabs dusted with a spicy herb seasoning and served with slices of tomatoes. Spice hung in the cool air, tickling her nostrils and watering her mouth. He took the bottles of malt and clicked the caps against each other. The tops popped off.

"That's a neat trick," she said, impressed.

His shoulder lifted in a shrug. "I learned it years ago in boarding school."

"It's not a very billionaire thing to do." She couldn't forget this man came from one of the richest families in West Africa and ran a company valued in billions of dollars.

"Are you saying being resourceful isn't a billionaire thing to do?" He raised one dark brow, his lips quirked as if he suppressed laughter.

"A resourceful billionaire would order someone else to open the cap, like the boy who was here earlier."

"Tonight, I'm just a man on a date—"

"We're not a date." She had to push the words past her dry throat caused by the husky edge to his voice.

"Aren't we?" He stretched out his arms across the table, reaching for hers. She pulled her hand down to her lap. If he touched her, she would lose all coherent thinking.

"No, Mark. This is just friends hanging out." She stared at the gentle waves lapping the shore, reflecting the silver of the moon.

"Okay. Tonight, I'm just a man hanging out with a beautiful friend. The billionaire is locked away until tomorrow morning." He pulled back his hands and unwrapped his parcel. "Or would you rather have the billionaire?"

She whipped her head around, the coolness in his voice unsettling her. "I never said that."

"Perhaps not. But I would like to hear you say it. Who would you rather be with right now? Mark, the billionaire, or Mark, the man?"

His hands stilled, his gaze riveted on her, as if her answer would be critical to him.

Yes, she admired Mark, the billionaire. He had so many business qualities she wanted to emulate. But right here, right now, this man sitting in front of her called to her like no other man ever had. After a stressful week, he made her laugh, her mind relaxed, and her body that had lain dormant for five years awoke.

"I would rather have Mark, the man," she blurted out.

A glorious smile spread across his face. "I'm glad to hear that."

He took a bite of his *suya*. Her focus glued to his kissable lips and rippling throat as he chewed and swallowed. She gulped, suddenly wishing he had kissed her in the car.

"You do know that I'm not going to kiss you if you eat onions."

Oh my God, what did I just say out loud? Somebody shoot me now.

Her face heated up as his lips widened and he flashed a set of white teeth.

He started picking out the onions from his *suya* and piling them at the corner of the wrapping. "We can't have that now, can we?"

"I didn't mean to say that. Sorry."

"Don't be sorry for speaking your mind with me, sweetheart. Moreover, I'm glad you said it. I don't want any excuses when I kiss you later."

Oh, God! She groaned inwardly and lowered her head to eat. He chuckled.

They ate in silence for a little while. The sound of the lapping sea waves and people talking and laughing on the beach kept them company.

"So, tell me. You mentioned you are not in the dating market? I checked and from all accounts, you are single. Otherwise, I wouldn't have asked to see you."

Lifting her head, their gazes connected. His eyes glinted with intensity. Her breath caught in her throat and she turned away again, concerned about his effect on her. One minute he made her laugh. The next, he had the ability to stare at her as if he wanted to unwrap her soul.

How did he do it? Mark, the joker who made her laugh, was easier to cope with than Mark, the inquisitor.

"Faith, talk to me. I really want to get to know you better."

She sighed. "The truth is that I'm not like you, or perhaps your usual girlfriends. I mean, you change girlfriends as often as I visit hairdressers. Whereas I...I haven't been in a relationship since when I did my youth service."

"Why? You're a very attractive woman. I don't get it," he said as he rolled up his now empty paper and took out his handkerchief from his pocket.

"Hold on." Faith reached in her bag and pulled out her pack of wet wipes. "I keep these in my bag as they come in handy sometimes."

"Thank you." He took a sheet. "I always wonder what women carry in their oversize bags that weigh a ton. Now I know one of it."

She laughed. "Well, you have to be prepared for any eventuality."

"I guess you do. I'll take that for you." He reached for her empty paper wrapper. "I'll find a bin and get rid of these."

He walked off and Faith used her time alone to think about his question. Did she really want to share something this intimate with him? Perhaps sharing it would make him understand why she couldn't be with him, and he would finally give up on any thoughts of dating her.

An ache bloomed in her chest at the idea of not seeing Mark again. He was great company. He made her smile, laugh, and feel like a woman. He also made her feel exposed, and that was somewhere she didn't want to go.

Mark came back and sat beside her again. "You're not trying to avoid my question, by any chance, are you?"

He took her hand but she pulled it back and balled it up on her thigh. She didn't want any physical contact. He would just wear her resolve away.

"No. I'm not avoiding your questions." She paused and exhaled. "I haven't dated because I've been so focused on my career and some of the men I've met are afraid of a career woman like me. I'm not very good girlfriend material."

"Nonsense," he said. "Why would you say such a thing?"

She stared at the lapping waves before turning back to Mark. "I've been accused of being frosty."

"You've got to be kidding me." He raised his brow and she shook her head. "The woman who kissed me back in Joburg blazed with such heat, I can't forget her.

He leaned forward and feathered her cheek with his index fingertip, leaving a trail of prickling skin.

"Seriously?" Delight bubbled inside her at his words.

"Absolutely." His grin filled with intent and he winked. "A man who can't raise your passion is obviously not for you."

"Perhaps," she replied. "But there were others who would rather have someone they can boss about and who's going to stay home and bear children."

His dark eyes caught the glint of the moon as he watched her intently. He didn't say anything immediately, as if thinking about her words.

"Are you saying you have no desire to have children?"

She shivered in disgust. "The last thing I want is to become a baby-making factory for a man who thinks that's all I'm worth."

"Woah. I'm sure no man wants to turn you into that," he said, raising his hands defensively.

"Try telling that to my father," she snapped.

She'd grown so riled up; she stood and stomped off down the beach. Her shoes sank into the sand from her heavy steps. She bent over and yanked them off her feet, holding them in her hand. The warm grains of sand between her toes had a soothing effect on her body and anger.

She hadn't walked very far when she felt Mark's presence beside her. He didn't say anything as he strolled beside her. She stopped and looked him over.

"Whatever you're going to say, don't."

He responded by making the zipping gesture across his lips, locking it, and throwing away the key. Laughter bubbled in her chest but she clamped it down, not ready to let him soothe her. He'd taken off his shoes and stood barefoot in the sand, shoes in hand, too.

"Why are your shoes off?" she asked, her tone guarded.

He did a mime of rummaging for something in the air and picked an item, which turned out to be the imaginary key he used to unzip his mouth.

"You know, I gotta act like the natives," he said in a mock Italian accent à la Don Corleone.

The laughter she'd been holding back burst out of her lips and she bent over as her ribs hurt from her squeals. When she finally lifted her head, he still had a glint of humour in his eyes.

"You know you're unreformable."

"I know, but sweetheart, you love me, right?"

"I won't go that far." She looked him up and down, still amused.

"Okay, perhaps you like me."

She shrugged. "A little."

"It's more than a little." He put his hand under her chin and tilted her head up. His eyes had lost the humour and grown intense.

"Admit it." His voice had acquired a soothing honey quality.

Everything else faded, leaving just the two of them standing on the moonlit beach. She swallowed, unable to move away. Her insides quivered.

"Yes, I like you more than a little, more than I should," she whispered in a breathless voice.

"And I like you a lot," he said as he pulled her close and moulded her body against hers. "A lot more than I should."

His lips descended on her, his teeth pulling her bottom lip into his mouth as he sucked on it. A spike of pleasure coursed through her body, her heart rate jumped. Rough and warm, his tongue skimmed the outside of her mouth and tunnelled into her welcoming mouth.

She moaned and he swallowed it. Her body responded as if this was where she belonged. Right here. In his arms. Their tongues tangled as he made love to her with his mouth, one of his hands on the rounded part of her bottom, and the other tugging at the short strands at the nape of her neck.

She should stop this, be outraged that he would kiss her. But her body enjoyed this swirl of emotions running through her. She'd never felt anything like it. Not when she'd had her first kiss ever at the ripe age of eighteen. Or her other encounters with men. This felt right. Heavenly. Blissful. Like it was meant to be. Like Mark's body was built for hers and hers for his.

What a foolish thing to think? Then again, her actions *were* foolish. Otherwise, she wouldn't be standing on a public beach kissing a man that every other woman wanted. A man who was also a business rival!

That thought got her moving and she focused all her energy on her hands currently curled in his silk shirt and pushed him back. He released her, looking a little bemused.

"What's wrong?" he asked, his voice husky and seductive.

"We can't do this." She looked around, glad there was no one close by that could've seen them kissing.

"Are you worried about people seeing us?"

"Yes."

"Come on. Let's head back to the car. Better still, my apartment is not far from here."

"No." She took a deep breath. "That's not what I meant."

"What, then?" He frowned.

"I mean, we can't kiss or get involved. Not here on the beach or anywhere else. Not ever."

"You still haven't given me a good reason why not."

"But—"

He held up his hand to stop her from speaking.

"And before you give me the spiel about men wanting to chain you to the kitchen sink until you deliver a football team of kids, I'll have you know I'm not looking for a wife, child-bearing or not."

"I..." She opened her mouth and closed it.

"You're a beautiful woman." He moved closer again. His scent and heat washed over her. "I'd like to get to know you, date you, and perhaps even make love to you, if you'll let me."

She was so mesmerised she didn't say anything.

"I'll be sure to take precautions so there are no resulting babies that you're so worried about. So, will you let me?"

"I will lose my job," she said when she'd recovered herself.

"What?" His eyes widened and his body stiffened. "You'll lose your job for dating me?"

"We are business rivals, remember? Conflict of interest. I'll be accused of passing corporate secrets to you during our pillow talks or whatever."

"I run the same risks, too. I'm sure you can separate work from your personal life. "

"But you haven't got a job to lose. You're the boss. I'm not."

"Well, if they sack you, you can always come and work for me."

"No," she replied, her voice breathy. Bad enough seeing him on a personal level. But she didn't want to have to see him every day at work. She would never be able to cope.

His eyes narrowed and lines appeared on his forehead.

"I'm sure you're a good boss and all that," she rushed to add. "It's just that I love my job at City and I have plans of becoming MD in the not too distant future. I don't want anything like getting involved with you to screw it up."

He heaved a sigh. "I'm a reasonable and very patient man. I've had to be to get to this point in my business and personal life. I understand your fears and am willing to back off for now. But get one thing straight. I want you and I'm not going to give up. I just need to find a solution to your problem."

"You—" he pointed to her and back to his chest, "— and me, we're going to happen." He brushed his lips against her mouth. "And when we do, you'll see how great we can be together."

He strode back towards the car and she followed him, mulling his words over in her head.

That night, she dropped him over at his apartment. He gave her a brief kiss before she drove back to her house.

True to his words, he didn't ask her out again on a date. However, they saw each other on occasions and more often once Ebony and Felix announced their wedding. Mark would be the best man and Faith the maid of honour. Which meant they were thrown together again as they helped plan the wedding which was to take place at the end of the year.

The wedding came and went and she survived, just about. How they'd managed to keep their hands off each other throughout the party, she didn't know. On several occasions, she'd wished he would renege on his promise to leave her alone and just grab her and find some dark corner to make love to her.

Even after the wedding, it seemed they couldn't be away from each other. Felix had been in a car crash which left him in a coma. Faith had been spending more time with a distraught Ebony, who worried about Felix making a full recovery.

Ebony had taken to spending some nights in hospital. She had dark shadows under her eyes and looked like she'd lost a lot of weight.

"Are you eating, darling? I'm worried about you," Faith said to her friend as she brushed back strands of hair that had fallen on her face.

Ebony shrugged. "I can't seem to keep any food down these days. To be honest, I haven't been very hungry recently."

"But you've got to eat. You've lost a lot of weight. I don't want to have to visit two people in hospital."

Ebony just nodded.

"Tonight, I think you should go home, eat some food, and freshen up."

"No. I can't leave him."

"You have to eat some food, Ebony. Please."

Ebony's eyes shimmered as tears welled up in her eyes. "Can't you see it's my fault he is in here?"

"What are you talking about?" She put her hands on her Ebony's frail shoulders.

"It's the same thing that happened to Chidi and Dad. I'm cursed. Anyone close to me either ends up dead or injured."

"Don't say that." Faith pulled her into her arms as Ebony broke down in tears. She held her friend as she cried her heart out.

Faith's heart ached for Ebony. Just when she thought her friend's life had settled into a positive outlook, now she had to deal with the stress of a husband in hospital, and they still weren't sure when or if he'd make a full recovery.

Even she who hated the thought of marriage couldn't wish such a horrific start to one for even her worst enemy.

"Dear, it's not your fault that Felix is in hospital. You didn't know he was going to have an accident. No one could've seen that."

"It was our wedding night and we had an argument. Can't you see it's my fault? If he doesn't wake up, I'll never forgive myself."

"He *will* wake up," Faith consoled her. "You'll see."

Gradually, Ebony's sniffles calmed down. Faith waited for Ebony and dropped her off at home so that Kola, Felix's bodyguard, didn't have to leave his station outside his suite door.

Next time she was in hospital visiting, Mark was there. Even he seemed to have dark shadows under his eyes and it looked as if he hadn't been sleeping. She was so taken aback by how stressed he looked, her heart went out to him.

Before she knew it, she'd invited him over to her house. His eyes brightened at her invitation and he agreed. When she bid farewell to Ebony and drove home, Mark followed her in his car.

At her house, the gatekeeper opened the metal gates and she drove in and told him to allow the car behind to come in. Mark drove in and parked in the empty spare spot beside her vehicle.

She stepped out and waited for him to come out before opening her front door. She dropped her bag on the table in the hallway and kicked her shoes off, glad to be out of them after a long day in the office and then visiting Ebony.

Turning around, she nearly bumped into Mark. Her breath caught in her throat. He stood so close to her, head and shoulders taller. Imposing and handsome, even with the tiredness lining his face. She stepped back, but he reached out and pulled her into the circle of his arms. His chest expanded as he took a deep breath, her head tucked under his chin.

"God knows I've missed you," he whispered into her hair.

Surprised and speechless, she hugged him tight, glad to just be in his arms, his hard strength and spice comforting.

After a long moment, he loosened his arms. She took a step back and tilted her head back so she could see his face.

"Can I get you a drink?" she asked as she walked up the stair to the living room.

He followed behind her. "Yes, please. Something cool and refreshing."

Tossing aside the scatter cushions and lowered his body onto one corner of the upholstered sofa and stretched out his legs.

"You have a beautiful home," he said as he studied the room.

The white walls, although bare, provided the canvass for the rest of the fixtures—beech wood furniture, mint-coloured settees, velvety coral-covered cushions.

"Thank you." She smiled, warmth spreading inside her body at his compliment. She went into the kitchen, withdrew a bottle of fresh mango juice from the fridge, found a tall glass from one of the cherry oak wall cupboard and returned to the living room.

Mark had his head back and eyes closed. He looked so relaxed she didn't want to disturb him. Her heart warmed just seeing him like that. He was the first man she'd had in her house since she moved into it over a year ago. For some reason, she liked having him here now, and she could just stand there watching him.

"I know you're there."

His deep, tired voice jolted her.

Warmth spread across her chest. Smiling, she stepped forward and placed the items in her hands on a side table. "I was trying not to disturb you in case you were asleep."

"I can smell you."

"What?" She sniffed herself.

"Not like that." His low, husky laughter filled her living room and he angled his head to stare at her face. "You smell of sunshine and lavender. I love your scent."

Cool fingers coiled around her left lower arm and he tugged. She tumbled onto his firm lap.

"Mark!" She giggled.

"I can't resist touching you."

He released her and she shifted on the sofa to the other end.

"You have to resist." She smiled at him. "You promised. Anyway, let me get you something to eat."

"What I want to eat is right here." The corner of his lips curled in a devilish smile.

Her insides contracted at his heated gaze. She needed to get away from him before they both did something they'd regret.

"Well, tough. I'm offering you some *jollof* rice with chicken, instead," she said and ran off to the kitchen as his laughter reverberated around her house.

CHAPTER FOUR

The retreat into the kitchen didn't last very long. At least, it didn't seem that way to Faith. Her heart pounded as she warmed up the food she'd prepared already, the tension in her stomach increasing.

Perhaps it hadn't been a good idea inviting Mark over to her house. Her body's reaction to his close proximity veered on crazy and she couldn't seem to calm it down.

Still, how could she have ignored the weariness that seemed to hang on his shoulders and the tension tightening his back muscles? They all seemed to have disappeared once he stepped into her place.

No. She was glad he came here. She wanted to be the one to soothe his worries, to let him know there was someone here for him as support outside of his immediate family. She was family, too, Ebony being like a sister to her.

Her home arrangement lay on split levels. The living room and dining room were on the first floor, the kitchen and guest bathroom on the lower floor, and bedrooms with en-suite bathrooms at the top level.

Faith returned upstairs with the food on a tray and set it on the dining table.

"Come on." She popped her head round the door of the living room to find Mark still sprawled on her sofa and scrolling through TV channels but not settling on any.

No matter how exhausted he appeared, he moved with grace and lithe as he straightened and joined her at the door. His hand settled on her lower back, warm and light. Possessive, yet not suffocating.

The gesture provided the option for her to move away from his touch. She didn't. Somehow, she liked his tactile nature, loved the contact even if she dreaded the implication. He made her feel as if he couldn't help but hold onto her, as if she mattered to him.

He pulled out a chair for her and waited until she sat down before moving to his own seat.

"You know you didn't have to go to all this trouble," he said when he sat down and she started dishing out rice onto his plate.

"Of course I had to. You told me you hadn't eaten anything today since breakfast."

"But I'm fine. I would've picked up something on the way home if I needed."

"Yes, you could've, but that would be more takeaway. A home-cooked meal is much better."

"Yes, you're right. This is delicious. Although I have to confess, I have a cook at home, so I don't always eat out."

"You have a cook?" She crinkled her face in a frown. "Why?"

"I do have to eat, and as you said, home-cooked food is sometimes best."

"Why don't you cook yourself? Don't tell me you can't cook."

"I run a multi-billion dollar business. My time is much better spent on other things than cooking."

Her spine stiffened and his frown deepened.

"So when you get married, do you expect your wife to do the cooking?"

"Of course. She'll be home more often than I'll be, taking care of our children. So it's expected."

"Hmmm." Faith grunted. Her nostrils flared and she glared at him. So angry, she didn't speak. *Couldn't* speak.

"What?" he asked as if he didn't understand why she would be upset.

She shook her head and lifted her glass of water to take a sip.

"I mean, women are known to be much better at cooking." He shrugged.

"Some of the best chefs in the world are men," she retorted. "Have you thought of that?"

"Yes, but in those cases, they do it for business. When they come home, I'm sure each one of them would still like to eat food cooked by their wives."

"Oh," she fumed. "You can be so arrogant and chauvinistic sometimes."

She put her cutlery down and crossed her arms over her chest.

"You're mad at me because I said I want to eat food cooked by my wife."

"No. Don't pretend you don't know the subliminal message your words deliver. Women should be at home while men go out to work."

"If that's what you think I mean, then why am I here with you? You're hardly housewife material."

"I'd like to know, too." She pushed back her chair and stood, ready to walk away from the dining table.

Firm fingers grabbed her wrist, held her still.

"I'm sorry. I shouldn't have said that." He sighed, the tired sound hanging in the air. "I guess this whole thing with Felix is making me lose my sense of humour."

She puffed out a breath and turned around. "I'm sorry, too. I brought you here to help soothe you, not rile you up. I really need to pipe down on the whole feminist propaganda, don't I?"

She lowered her body into the seat, took another deep breath and changed the topic. "How are you coping with everything?"

"It hasn't been easy. Trying to run my business and oversee Felix's, as well, and worrying about my parents. My dad isn't dealing very well with Felix being in hospital. He has a special fondness for my older brother, and I'm worried if Felix doesn't make it through—"

"Don't even think it. Felix will get through this. He's a fit young man. Of course he'll wake up."

"I hope so. We all hope so. Even Tony, who we never see, has been volunteering to help out."

"Oh yeah, your younger brother. I saw him at the wedding. Doesn't he work for one of your businesses?"

"No. He's an 'artist'." Mark drew invisible quotes in the air with both hands and chuckled. "Tony fancies himself as a movie mogul."

Faith leaned back, the derisive words hitting home. It reminded Faith of how her father had laughed when she'd said she wanted to run businesses instead of getting married.

"A woman's place is in the home not in an office."

Faith shivered at the remembered words.

"If making movies is what he wants to do, you should let him," Faith said in a serious tone. She knew what if felt like to be told she couldn't be what she wanted to be because of other people's expectations.

"We're letting him do what he wants. I would simply like one of his ventures to actually make some money instead of him coming to ask for more investments."

"I'm sure he'll surprise you one of these days."

"I look forward to that day." He lifted his glass of mango juice in a toast. "Thank you for a lovely meal."

"You're welcome." She started clearing the table.

"Let me do it." Standing, he grabbed her hand and stopped her. "Go and put your feet up."

"It's okay. I don't mind. You're my guest."

"Look, I'm hardly a guest. Moreover, you were the one berating me earlier. So let me help."

"Okay, we'll both do it."

She took the tray and he carried the glasses down after her. In the kitchen, she washed up and he dried the dishes, then she showed him where to put them. Seeing him in her kitchen reinforced the growing feelings she had for him. Something about him there, his sleeves rolled up his arms, the two of them relaxed, laughing and chatting in domestic bliss.

Would it be really wrong to have this daily? To see him like this, to spend the time with him without complications? She shook her head and wiped down the work surface as Mark put the last dishes away.

"Can I taste you now?" he whispered in a low gruff voice, the warm air from his breath lifting the hairs on the back of her head.

His chest pressed against her shoulders, his erection hot and hard and burning into her back.

"Mark." His name came out like a soft prayer on her lips, her core contracting in expectation.

Was she saying yes or no? She wasn't sure anymore. The only certainty she could rely on was how her body responded to his request. Aroused.

Soft lips brushed the edge of her ear lobe and a wet, rough tongue licked a fiery path on the inside. Panting, she puffed air in and out of her open mouth as her body trembled uncontrollably.

Fight this... Why?

Rational thinking flew out of the open window of the kitchen as his mouth continued its devastating trail down her neck.

One second she was trying to collect her thoughts; the next, she was staring into his eyes and suddenly wishing she hadn't. His need burned bright in his dark irises, a blazing star of craving in the midnight sky. She got sucked right into orbit, pulled into his soul.

When his lips met hers, his hunger fuelled hers, flame to gasoline. Erupting into a bundle of sensation encased within his shell of hot, hard, arousing muscles, she lost all sense of herself.

His lips sucked and pulled, his teeth nipped and grazed.

Fisting her hands in the soft fabric of his shirt, she clung on, wanting to feel him inside as well as outside. Everywhere. All at once.

Before she was fully aware of her actions, she'd climbed his sturdy legs, wrapping hers around his hips. A guttural sound registered in her lust-riddled mind as the ridge of his erection lined up with her damp knickers, her skirt now riding up her thighs.

Had the groan come from her or Mark?

With one hand on her hip, he lifted her until she sat on the worktop and he stood between her legs. She churned her hips, grinding her sex against the hard bulge of his arousal. He pulled the hem of her blouse out of her skirt and pushed it up over her torso. Her nipples, already taut, strained in her satin bra, her breasts heavy and sensitive.

"My...you're beautiful."

His voice came out filled with awe and a deep sexiness that vibrated in her core. He took a nipple into his warm, wet mouth, sucking deeply.

She cried out in a long moan, her body writhing beneath his as she bowed off the surface. She hovered so close to a climax. And he seemed to know it. He repeated the action on her other breast.

"Mark!" She screamed out his name as her orgasm hit her, heavy, drenching, and devastating, her whole body rocking for seconds on end.

He wrapped his hands around her and held her to him, nuzzling her neck until she calmed and reality hit her.

What did they just do? What did *she* just do?

She stiffened in his arms. He must have sensed her tension. He leaned back, looking at her face, but she couldn't meet his gaze.

"Faith—"

"Mark, don't." She lifted her hand to stop him. Too embarrassed to listen to his words. What else was there to say apart that it shouldn't have happened? She pushed herself up and slid away from him, rolling down her skirt and blouse to a semblance of decency. "It's been a long day and we are both tired."

"I'll take it that's not an invitation to finish what we just started."

"I'm sorry, Mark. I shouldn't have let it get this far."

Gosh! She'd even climaxed, and they both still had their clothes on. All he'd done was kiss her and suck on her nipples and she'd disintegrated like a virginal teenager.

"The hell it shouldn't have happened." He took a step towards her, eyes blazing with passion. "You want me as much as I want you. The sooner you admit it, the better for both of us."

Then he swivelled and departed from the kitchen, walking up the stairs.

She gripped the table, sucking in gulps of air, trying to calm her trembling body. Who was she kidding? She'd wanted him. Still wanted him. If he came back and touched her the way he had, she would fall apart again. She would let him take her any way he wanted. It all showed the kind of effect he had on her body.

His keys jingled in their bunch as he came downstairs. With still trembling legs, she walked out to meet him in the hallway. He had his jacket over his left arm and his car keys in his right hand.

"Sweetheart, I care about you enough to give you time to wrap your head around what just happened between us." Heated black eyes stared at her, making her heart stutter. "But be assured that next time, I won't be walking away."

He opened her front door and stepped out.

From that day onwards, she avoided Mark. A cowardly thing to do, but the only way she knew she could resist him. If she ever stood in the same room as him again, she wouldn't be able to say no to him.

Fortunately, Felix woke from the coma and in a few days, returned home so she had no reason to visit the hospital again. Mark made no special effort to seek her out. He didn't call or visit her at the office or at home.

Truthfully, his absence niggled at her. She missed his company and his humour.

Later that year, Ebony gave birth to a baby boy and Faith was named godmother. She dreaded the day of the christening because Mark had been named the godfather, along with his brother, Tony.

However, she shouldn't have been worried. Mark barely gave her more than a perfunctory glance and a quick hello. She didn't realise how much she'd missed him until she stood next to him in the chapel aisle without getting his usual smile directed at her.

After the blessing at the church, they went back to Felix and Ebony's house, an invitation just for the close family. Ebony dragged Faith to the upstairs lounge and left Felix and Mark with their parents and her mum who were fussing over the baby for a while.

"You look great for a new mum," Faith said when she sat down in the sofa, glad to be away from having to stare at Mark. "All glowing and lovely."

"Thank you," Ebony said, pouring out the drinks that Bisi, their housekeeper, had left on the coffee table. "I didn't know I'd love being a parent so much but it's fantastic."

"Alex is so gorgeous and well-behaved, too. I can't believe he didn't cry once throughout the christening."

"He is adorable, isn't he?" Ebony smiled as she took a sip of her drink. "I didn't know I could love anyone the way I love him."

"I'm so happy for you. I'm glad you and Felix finally sorted everything out."

Ebony nodded. "Yes, this brings me to what I wanted to talk to you about." She paused. "What is going on between you and Mark?"

"Why. What has he said?" Faith asked defensively as she cupped her glass in both hands.

"He hasn't said anything, and that's my point. He is being closed off. Did something happen between the two of you?"

Faith shrugged but didn't say anything.

"Come on, talk to me. You know, as godmother to Alex, you're not allowed to keep secrets from me."

"Okay. I'll talk." She took a deep breath. "Something happened—well, almost happened...has been happening. Oh, I don't know."

She lifted her hands up in frustration. This whole thing with Mark drove her insane.

"We can't be together," she said at last.

"Why not?" Ebony asked.

"Because...because of my job." Right now, that reason didn't sound so foolproof.

"Your job? I don't get it."

"He works—runs a rival firm. I'm director of Strategy at City. Getting involved with him amounts to a conflict of interest."

"Oh, come on. The two of you are adults. You're hardly going to be sharing confidential corporate information with each other."

"I—"

"Moreover, you've been doing great things at City and they should know you'd never do anything that would mess up the business."

"I know. But think about the scandal that will ensue if it gets into the press. It could be damaging to City."

"Faith, you worry too much," Ebony said. "If you like him like I think you do, I'm sure the two of you would find a way around any problems that arise."

"I don't know," she said staring down at her hands, her shoulders slumped. "I think he's gone off me. He's hardly said two words to me all day."

"He's just brooding. It's an Essien trait. He needs an incentive to snap out of it."

"I don't know, Ebony. Our relationship is not like what you have with Felix. The two of you love each other. You wanted to get married and stay together, in the end. Not like Mark and me."

"Oh, come on, Faith." Ebony leaned forward and took her hand. "I know you. Beneath all that 'girls run the world' façade, you still like what Felix and I have. And you can have it, too. If you loosen up a bit and let it happen."

"The truth is that I'm afraid. The way Mark makes me feel, no other man has made me feel that way. I lose myself whenever he's around."

"That's a good thing, Faith. You are usually so sure of yourself and where you're going in life with all your five-year plans." Ebony laughed. "Perhaps it's time you learned to just live life, without a plan, and see where it takes you."

"That's a scary thought."

"And you're a brave woman who's not afraid of facing lions in a boardroom. You can certainly deal with Mark and survive."

"Yes, I can." She said it more as a pep talk to herself than as a response to Ebony.

"So, what are you going to do about it?" Her friend curled her lips in a teasing smile.

"Oh, I think I know a way to make him take notice. I just need some time alone with him."

"There you are." Felix walked into the room, carrying the baby. "Alex needs a change."

"Okay." Ebony stood and went over to her husband.

Faith's skin prickled before she saw Mark had walked in behind Felix. She blinked a couple of times as she drank in the sight of him. He wore a taupe linen suit. In the fitted cut, he looked very striking, very masculine. Her chest tightened, butterflies fluttering low in her belly.

"Why don't you help me change Alex," Ebony said to Felix but she looked back at Faith and gave her a wink.

"You need me?" Felix looked a little bemused.

"Yes, there's something I want to show you in our bedroom." Ebony gave her husband a knowing look and nodded towards Mark and Faith.

"Ah, of course." Felix walked out of the room with one last glance at his brother.

Faith sashayed over to the mini bar in the corner, swaying her hips provocatively. Out of her league trying to be sexy, but there existed no other way for her to thaw out the cold Mark.

She leaned her hip against the bar and turned to face him. His gaze appeared heated and he couldn't seem to take his eyes off her. Her heart pounded as she lifted her glass to her lips before taking a sip of the lemonade.

"Would you like a taste?" She tilted her glass towards him.

From the flare of passion in his eyes, he knew she was offering more than a sip of fizzy drink. He'd used the same phrase before he'd kissed her in her kitchen. Now, she wanted him to kiss her again.

Tension oozed off his body.

"You're playing with fire," he said as he took a step towards her.

"I'm not playing," she replied, her gaze hooked on his.

"A taste won't be enough," he growled, his tone husky as he took another step.

"Take as much as you want," she said, her voice now hoarse and low as the whoosh of rushing blood in her ears got louder.

"I want everything...I want all of you."

He stood in front of her but didn't touch her. He shoved his hands in his pockets as if he fought not to reach for her. The arc of electricity between them sizzled. Body trembling, she didn't know how long she could stand there, glad at least the bar propped her up.

"Okay."

She couldn't believe she was agreeing to this. But as Ebony had pointed out, she only had one life and as lovely as it was, there seemed to be something missing at the moment.

Mark.

He smiled for the first time that she'd seen that day. His gaze swept over her from head to toes before returning to her lips. Was he going to kiss her now? Her body vibrated with expectation.

"Did you bring your car?" she asked, taking another sip.

"Yes. Why?" One dark eyebrow quirked up.

"Mine's in for a service and I think we should get to your place. It's closer." Heart pounding, she slipped past him to go pick up her bag. He grabbed her arm, his thumb brushing against her skin.

"Faith, there's no reason to rush."

"Really? You've waited a year to have me, and now when I'm offering myself, you still want to wait some more?" She raised her brow.

"You've got a point there. I'll tell Felix we're heading off."

CHAPTER FIVE

Saying goodbye to everyone took a little longer than Faith anticipated. She got into a conversation with Mrs. Duru about the annual charity fundraising event for the NGO that Ebony's mum oversaw. Mark stood not far from where she'd been made to sit, chatting with his father. She avoided eye contact with him, not wanting the others to know something went on between them. But her body buzzed with the anticipation and it was all she could do not to fidget in her chair.

Her skin prickled—he must've been staring at her. She always sensed it when his focus landed on her. From the corner of her eye, she saw Mark head towards the exit. He glanced at her and winked as he smiled. Her cheeks heated.

"Mum, I've really got to go now," she said to Mrs. Duru, trying to rush her. "I'm going to call you and arrange to come over so that we can chat about what we need to do this year for the fundraising."

"Of course. You do that." Mrs. Duru waved her on.

She bid quick goodbyes to Mark's parents. Ebony walked her to the door.

"I see that whatever tactics you used on Mark worked," her friend said as they stepped into the dusky evening. "He looks like a cat about to get his cream."

Faith grinned. "Oh, I hope so."

Ebony giggled. "Have fun. We'll catch up sometime during the week."

Mark held the door of his low, sleek Aston Martin sports car. As she got into the passenger seat, his palm brushed her back. The touch felt so light that, for a second, she thought she'd imagined it. But the heated gaze he gave her seemed filled with such promise. The anticipation in her belly knotted tighter.

Ebony and Felix stood outside while Mark started the car and reversed. Through the open window and above the soft purring sound from the car, Faith heard Felix say, "There is something going on between those two."

Ebony's soft laughter floated into the car. "There will be, if my girl knows what's good for her."

A smile played on her lips and she turned to see if Mark had heard the comment. His lips were curled in a sexy smile but he concentrated on the road as the windows slid up noiselessly.

They both sat silently while Mark manoeuvred through the early evening traffic out of Ikoyi. They drove down leafy avenues, past colonial style mansions behind high walls and gated properties that reeked of old money and elitism.

She earned good money but even on her income, she couldn't afford property in this little strip of Lagos without breaking the bank. Yet, her best friend and her husband lived in one of those houses. And now she was headed to another equally posh area in Victoria Island with Mark.

Relaxing back into her soft leather bucket seat, she watched the confident way he drove. Something incredibly sexy about seeing a man handle a powerful car so assuredly. His light grip on the steering wheel, flicking it one way or the other depending on the direction they were going, as if the car was totally under his command, obeying his every whim.

She now understood why some women would have sex in a car. Sports cars and powerful men were a recipe to get any woman's knickers wet and hers were soaking. Already so turned on, sitting still in the car was becoming a problem.

"How long to get to yours?" she asked, suddenly impatient.

"Not long," he replied, giving her a quick glance. "Have you changed your mind?"

"No. I want you. I just don't know if I can wait till we get there."

The quick, sexy glance he gave her before he gunned the engine and drove faster only added to her already aroused state of mind. Neither of them spoke again until they arrived at his apartment five minutes later.

As expected, the building was gated. The uniformed security man nodded as Mark drove in and down the curved driveway. He parked the car in the underground car park and got out before she could, opening the door for her. Rows of expensive cars doted the car lot.

The only people who could afford to live in these apartments being the young, über rich Nigerians or expatriates who earned in dollars and worked for international companies.

This time around, surprise filled her when he didn't attempt to touch her as they walked into the marbled foyer of his apartment building, or even after they entered the shiny, brushed metal lift on the way up to the penthouse level.

Tension dangled heavy in the air as they stared at each other, his gaze never wavering while he stood barely inches away from her. Shallow breaths filled her lungs with his scent—spicy and masculine—calling to her to lean forward. But she took his cue and held her body still, though it vibrated with the need to be close to him.

The way he stared at her, her nipples pebbled, turning to stiff points, her breasts full and heavy with need, seeking his attention. She ran the tip of her tongue over her lips, reminding herself to breathe in and out.

She used the time to sweep her gaze up and down his body. He'd taken his linen jacket off, leaving just his white silk shirt with the buttons undone halfway down, his broad chest filling it out and tapering into his trousers.

Hunger radiated from him, his body coiled like a predator waiting for the right opportunity to pounce. Muscles tightened on his shoulders, his hands clenched and unclenched beside him, as if he struggled to keep his hands off her.

His gaze slid over her body in a slow caress and all her nerve endings tingled in anticipation of the promise that lay in his irises.

With her eyes, she followed the line to where a bulge curved his trousers. Her pulse rate sped up as she realised he'd grown hard and aroused because of her. She'd been used to having intellectual prowess over men and always suppressed her sexual side.

Her lips curled in a smile, knowing she had some sexual leverage over Mark, even if it would be temporary. A man like Mark never stayed with a woman for long, if the reports and pictures of him in the news media were anything to go by.

Then again, Mark wasn't included in her five-year plan. He wasn't part of her future. So it shouldn't matter to her. Somewhere in her heart, a light dimmed at the thought. Sadness hovered over her shoulders, pushing them down.

At that moment, the elevator pinged.

Mark leaned forward and grabbed her arm, the first time he'd touched her since they'd left Ebony's house, and practically dragged her through the doors. She barely had time to take in her surroundings. Her heart pounded so loudly, the rush of blood between her ears drowned out every other sound.

Before she knew it, he had shoved her against the wall of his apartment. The door hadn't fully shut behind when he had her flat against the concrete, his body crushing hers as his lips slammed down on hers.

His hand grabbed the short strands of her hair and tugged her head back as he slanted his sensuous lips across hers. No finesse in this kiss; no gentleness, either.

Passion flared as soon as their lips connected and his tongue plunged into her mouth in a rhythm that mimicked the actions she hoped would be repeated in her nether region. Pure animalistic hunger, a result of the months of restraint between them that could no longer be held back.

Suddenly out of control, she clawed at his shirt, wanting some skin-to-skin contact with him. She managed to pull the hem of his shirt up and her hands made contact with solid and hot stomach muscles.

A loud groan erupted from Mark as he lifted his head, both of them panting to get air into their lungs.

"Sweetheart, you drive me crazy."

His voice thrummed thick with lust. He ran the pads of his fingers over her breasts still encased in her bra and blouse. More sensation zinged through her body. But she still wasn't satisfied. She wanted more. More body contact without the clothes between them.

She was already going mad with lust. The fire burning within her needed to be tamed before it burned her up.

"I can't wait, Mark," she managed to moan out in a breathless voice. She moved her hand up to his shoulders, clinging onto his neck as she climbed him with her legs. "Hurry."

He didn't hesitate. He pinned her to the wall, stepping between her legs as he held on to her hip. His other hand slid up her thigh, pushing up her skirt to meet the lace edge of her underwear. His fingers brushed her sex through the damp lace, feeling the evidence of her desire.

"Mark," she cried out in pleasure, canting her hips into his touch, her body primed and ready to burst. The sound of his zipper sliding open drew her attention down his body again as she hooked one leg over his hip.

"Hang on," he said as he reached behind and pulled something out of his back pocket. He took a foil of condom out of his wallet and tossed the leather aside. Using his teeth, he tore the wrapper off and sheathed himself in latex.

Seeing his hard length ready for her reminded her she still had her knickers on. In fact, they were both still fully clothed, albeit in a state of disarray. Before she had time to do anything, he had his fingers between her legs. The sound of lace tearing ripped through the air and then he was spreading her thighs apart and nudging her wet entrance.

He thrust in. Her body bowed off the wall. The shock on her system came as both pain and pleasure. She hadn't had a man inside her for a long time. Years. And Mark felt both alien and blissfully snug at the same time.

"Faith."

Her name sounded like a groan, a prayer, on his lips.

"Mark...please." She wriggled, wanting more of him.

"Relax, sweetheart. Otherwise, this will be over before we've started."

His hand invaded the little space between them and his fingers parted her lower lips. He caressed her nub, eliciting a cry of pleasure from her. She leaned her head on the hard surface behind and closed her eyes, savouring the sensations running riot inside her.

He slid out until just his broad head caressed her inner walls. Then he thrust back in, this time to the hilt, the metal buckle of his belt rubbing against her inner thigh.

She opened her eyes. Mark had his head tilted back, neck arched, shoulders straining, arms bunched, sweat glistening on his forehead and hands gripping her hips tightly. He looked magnificently beautiful in that moment, his raw passion glinting in his dark eyes. Her heart clenched just as her inner walls tightened.

They hadn't even turned the lights on in the hallway. The only light came through the floor-to-ceiling window, from the outdoor lights and night sky.

Face wrung in a fierce expression, he looked down and started thrusting.

"Is this what you wanted?" he grunted, sliding out and thrusting in.

"Yes... Oh...Yes!" The words whooshed out of her with each of his thrusts.

The sound of their panting filled the air around them. He rolled his hips, stroking her insides as well as her outsides.

"I've wanted you for so long," he said as he brushed his lips on her chin. He nipped her flesh before soothing the sting with his rough tongue.

"Wanted this." He thrust in again, stroking her deeply. Perfectly. "Wanted more than this."

It was all she could do not to tremble with pleasure, her whole body primed and racing towards a climax within reach.

It seemed he knew how close she was. His lips caressed her cheeks.

"Give me all you've got, sweetheart," he whispered in a low voice close to her ear, the warm air stroking her already sensitive skin.

She dug her heels into the back of his thighs, matching his strokes with each cant of her hips, meeting him. Between the way his length loved her insides and his fingers massaged her outer sex, she climaxed in a slow, pained moan, shivering with pleasure as she whimpered his name, her body clenching in ripples after ripples of a totally overwhelming orgasm.

"You are the most beautiful creature," he said in a hoarse voice before kissing her roughly, his tongue marauding in her mouth.

He increased the speed of his strokes and she held on as his measured drives kept her hot and wanting again. Her core tightened, hungry all over for more of him.

"You feel so good," she said, loving his hot, hard, smooth glide in and out.

She couldn't believe she'd held out so long from experiencing him like this. He felt more than good. Like he was made for her and her for him. Though their actions at the moment seemed to be based more on instinct than planning, unlike her usual activities. But she loved this spontaneity and the freedom flowing excitedly in her veins.

"It's you, sweetheart." He kissed her, his left hand tightening on her hip while the other squeezed her left breast, sparking a new orgasm to life. He took her in long, deep plunges, dragging her climax to new heights.

"It's all you," he said as he quickened his pace before his whole body tensed and he threw his head back and came in hot, hard spurts inside her, his body racked in powerful shudders. He groaned her name, his neck muscles wound tight, the intensity of his coming oozing off his bunched up shoulders and arms.

Both their rasping breaths filled the air and it took a few moments before the shudders in their bodies calmed enough. He leaned forward, resting his sweat-streaked forehead against hers.

"I'm sorry we didn't make it to the bed." He tightened his hold on her, still braced against the door. "I've never lost control like that before."

"I'm not sorry." Thank goodness they had the concrete structure to prop them up. Otherwise, she would have slid to the floor. Her legs had suddenly turned into dead weights.

"I'm glad you lost control with me," she said with a smile. The first time she'd done anything like it. "It's my first time of having sex against a wall. And I like it."

He chuckled as he nuzzled her neck. "I aim to please. Now, let's get to the bed and do it properly, this time without any clothes on."

She giggled as he scooped her up and she wondered how he had the energy after all that. She wouldn't have been able to walk properly herself. She clung on to his neck, taking in the heady scent of Mark and sex.

Luckily, his bedroom wasn't far down the hallway. The bed he laid her on was covered in chocolate silk sheets, soft to the touch and smelling of fresh laundry, and massive enough to accommodate a basketball team. The room itself looked larger than her living room, decorated in varying natural brown tones of fabric and wood.

Mark towered above her, hands on his hips. His dark eyes glimmered with such intensity, a black hole that sucked her right in, her heart thudded loudly.

"I don't think I've ever seen you more beautiful," he said in a gruff voice.

Huh? She lifted one brow in disbelief and looked down at her body.

Dishevelled—her rumpled linen skirt rode up her bare hips, her lace knickers torn, a button missing from her silk blouse. Not to mention that her hair must probably be all over the place since he'd been running his fingers through the strands and the back had been crushed against the door. Was he pulling her leg or what?

"You must need glasses, then," she said, sure he must've been joking. "I'm rumpled up."

"Yes, so beautifully rumpled." He rolled off the used condom, knotted it, and tossed it into the brushed steel waste paper bin leaning against the wall by the door. "Do you know how long I've waited to see you this rumpled? Every time I see you, you're always so composed, so prim and proper. I've wanted to see passion blaze in your eyes, wanted to see you finally let go."

Leaning over, he stroked her lips in a brief kiss. His masculine spice filled her lungs, stirring the burnt-out embers of her lust.

CHAPTER SIX

Faith's cheeks heated and she half-laughed, half-coughed in a self-conscious manner. Her body still tingled as if it finally woke up from a long sleep. A really long sleep.

"Of course, I wasn't expecting that finally getting you to loosen up will get me so out of control I was going to explode within seconds like a teenager."

How could he say that or even expect her to believe it? In the past year, he hadn't exactly been lonely. Unlike her. He shouldn't pretend this was more than it was. Sex. Lust. That's all they had.

She rolled over, trying to cover herself up in a semblance of decency. The thought of him with other women had her heart clenching tightly.

"If I believe that, I'll believe anything." She pulled herself up and away from him. "You forget that your pictures have been splashed over the papers with different women hanging on your arms this past year."

The mattress depressed as he sat on the edge. Tendrils of his heat curled around her. Breathing saturated her lungs with his spice. Need bubbled in her veins. She closed her eyes, hating the tightness in her chest.

Remember, this is just sex. It doesn't matter how many women he's been with this past year.

Bullshit. Her hands clenched into fists, tightening on the seams of her clothes.

"Yes, I've attended events with women all because you refuse to be seen publicly with me. I would rather have had you as my escort on those occasions."

Fingers, steel bands, wrapped around her ankles and tugged. Eyes flying open, she gulped in air and slid down the bed on her back until her legs straddled his hips. One by one, he removed her shoes and massaged her bare feet. His fingers worked blissful magic. She purred, to her dismay.

"But I haven't had sex with another woman since I met you at that conference in Jo'burg."

Stunned by his admission, all she could say was, "Okay."

Relief washed over her body at his reassuring words and she didn't hide the smile that tugged the corners of mouth. A man as highly sexed as Mark had stayed celibate for a year for her. Euphoria, a heady drug, surged in her veins. The constriction around her chest loosened, rage replaced by delight, empowering her.

A dimple flashed on his cheek, his lips curled in a slow, confident smile. Masculine and erotic, semen glistened on the semi-hard erection jutting out of his open fly.

God, he's beautiful and sexy and virile. Magnificent. Between her thighs throbbed, a mixture of soreness and arousal. She wanted him again.

Her mouth watered. She'd never given head before. No time like right now to start. Pushing up on her elbows, she licked her lips and ran her sole over his erection.

His groan thrummed loud and vibrated through her, his shaft stiffening and lengthening immediately. She ran her tongue over her lips as she teased him with her foot.

"Let's get into the shower." His voice sounded hoarse as he stood up but seemed to wobble in place.

Her grin widened that she could be making him feel unsteady on his feet.

"I want to taste you," she teased, running her feet up and down his thigh.

"You won't taste much of me if I don't get a shower, just latex."

"Oh."

He unbuttoned his shirt and paused, wrinkling his brows.

"You've never tasted a man before, have you?"

Her cheeks heated and she looked away as she shrugged. A big grin spread across his face and he leaned over and scooped her up, giving her a long, intense, breath-stealing kiss.

"You're adorable," he said in a husky voice when he lifted his head.

"That makes me sound like a naive school girl," she said, bristling through the haze of lust spreading over her body.

"'Naive' and 'school girl' are three words I can never use to describe you. There is nothing school-girlish about these voluptuous curves of yours, and I think words like 'incredibly beautiful' and 'indomitable' describe you better."

Somehow, her brain skipped over all the other words and focused on the one that had her feeling self-conscious again. At five-foot–four-inches, she was hardly stick-thin. Her big breasts and behind had gotten her into trouble before, the reason why she hid them inside conservative clothing.

"Are you saying I'm fat?" She cocked her eyebrow.

He chuckled as he carried her into the bathroom.

"Fat? No. Curvy, shapely, luscious, buxom, and sexy? Hell, yes!"

Her smile widened. "Oh, you're good for a girl's ego." She giggled. She understood why so many women flocked to him. Mark was a charmer and like chocolate—an addiction she couldn't get rid of.

She'd been so distracted by him, she didn't realise what he was doing until he walked into the massive shower enclosure with wall-to-ceiling grey limestone tiles and overhead spotlights. The huge showerhead descended directly from the ceiling, water cascading down and splashing over both of them.

"Wh— what are you doing?" she spluttered, drenched in warm water. "We've still got our clothes on."

"I'm making sure you don't run tonight," he said as he let her body gently slide down until she stood in front of him.

Stunned, she remained there staring at him mouth agape, not sure whether to be angry or not. His shirt plastered against his chest, his trousers clung to his sturdy thighs, just as she was sure her own clothes now stuck wetly to her skin. She was learning so much about this man standing before her.

Lesson number one—Mark was a doer, in business and obviously, in his personal life. The gentle throbbing between her legs would be enough proof.

Lesson number two—he learned too quickly. After the incident in her kitchen the last time, he was unwilling to take the risk that she would want to end the night quicker than he wanted.

Lesson number three—he could read her too easily. She'd been hoping to get back home early and prepare for the new work week. Now, she didn't have the option. Mark had read her intentions even before they'd manifested, and he'd read her correctly. Never a good thing. When the time came, she wouldn't be able to outmanoeuvre him in negotiations if they ever faced off.

"That's no reason to ruin perfectly good clothes," she huffed, more annoyed with herself for being so easy to read than with him.

"It'll be taken care of by the laundry service and ready for you to wear in the morning," he said as he slipped his shirt off his arms and tossed it onto the stone-tiled floor.

"That means I have to stay here until the morning."

She said it more as a statement than a question. Not like she still had the choice, unless she wanted to go home wearing wet clothes.

"My point exactly. I'm sure I can find ways to keep you entertained until then."

He pulled his trousers all the way down and stepped out of them, repeating the same action with the shirt. He straightened and her jaw dropped.

She'd had an inkling he must be built well, but she still wasn't prepared for the specimen of caramel-skinned masculinity standing before her. She forgot to remove her own clothes as she gaped at his broad chest, muscular arms, and powerful, thick thighs as glistening water ran down his skin in rivulets. The result of all his hours in the gym showed. She practically salivated.

OMG! She hadn't had sex in close to five years and had lived without it. And yet, a few minutes with Mark and she had turned into a nymphomaniac.

"You keep looking at me that way and we'll be attempting a world record on shower sex." He growled the words out.

Picking her chin off the floor, she shut her mouth and pulled the rest of the buttons of her blouse through the holes.

Mark reached for her shoulders and peeled her blouse off her. His hand on her skin sparked her arousal. Her nipples puckered against the wet bra, poking above the crescent cup. She reached behind to take the bra off. Mark stopped her with his hand on her arm.

"Let me." The boyish dimple came back.

He unhooked the clasp and pivoted, chucking her top and bra to join his clothes on the floor. In the meantime, she tugged at the zipper of her skirt and yanked it down, pulling what remained of her ripped knickers, too, before stepping out of them.

Mark's low whistle bounced off the tiles as he sized her up, his heated gaze sliding over her skin like a caress, adding to the feel of warm water washing over her.

"Now, here's a woman designed to be adored."

Awe and heat battled in his gaze before he leaned forward and pumped some shower gel from the dispenser into his palm. He rubbed his hands together as if in glee and started massaging the foam onto her shoulders. The aromas of bergamot and sandalwood filled the enclosure, spicy and sexy, the scent she always associated with Mark. His shower gel, not cologne as she'd originally assumed.

Taking a deep breath, she relaxed into his touch as he continued rubbing her skin, moving around her breasts in a circular motion, down her belly. He squatted, soaping her legs in an up and down motion. He didn't linger between her legs and she was grateful.

"Turn around."

He stood and waited for her to move into place. He squirted more gel into his hand and focused on washing her back. Bracing her palms on the cool wall tiles, she closed her eyes and indulged in the luxury of having someone pamper her this way. Certainly another first.

"Can I wash your hair?" he asked.

She glanced behind her. He stood there, smiling and waiting for her confirmation. She nodded. Her hair was already wet.

"Although, it's going to look messy without a blow dryer," she added.

"I think I have a solution to that." He raked his fingers on her scalp and massaged it with both hands.

She exhaled and melted against the wall.

"Wow. You have magic fingers." She tilted her head into his touch. "This feels so good."

He finished off and tilted the showerhead to focus on her, rinsing the soap off her body. Facing him, she wanted to return the favour. She needed to get her hands on him.

"Now, it's my turn."

"You're welcome to have your wicked way with me." He grinned.

"I will."

She pumped gel into her hands like he'd done and started on his chest. He stood there confidently, hands down by his side, looking blatantly masculine and sexy while she massaged soap all over his body. His body felt hard, the light spread of short dark hairs on his chest giving his skin a rough, very male feel. She took her time, taking all of him in, learning all the contours and ridges of his muscles.

As she scrubbed his back, he leaned his head against the wall tiles, his hands also braced against it. His muscles relaxed beneath her fingers as she worked a massage over his back down to this firm butt cheeks. She couldn't resist grabbing on to them and squeezing. Mark groaned out loud.

Between her legs, her desire awakened and she throbbed for him. She wanted his hardness all over her as well as inside her again.

But she concentrated on giving his body the attention he'd given hers. After he was covered, she turned the showerhead on his back and rinsed him off. He straightened up and turned around.

She gasped at the sight of his raging hard-on, jutting upward towards his belly button.

"Oh, my," she said.

"You seem to have magic fingers yourself," he said.

"Oh, I better make good use of them, then." She reached for him, wrapping her fingers around his girth of muscles and veins. He pulsed in her hand, swelling and lengthening.

Mark inhaled sharply. She glanced up at him. His black eyes sparkled with heated intensity as if he couldn't keep his eyes off her and he waited to see what she would do next.

She pumped him a couple of times and leaned forward, flicking her tongue around the bulbous head. His groan deepened, encouraging her. Opening her lips, she swallowed the tip into her mouth, sucking as deeply as she could, her hand wrapped around the base.

She'd never done this before but she'd read enough books to know the basics. Was she doing it right? Flicking her eyes upward, the image Mark projected locked her breath in her lungs.

His head tilted back onto the tiled wall, his eyes closed, and his hands clenched and unclenched at his sides, as if he stood at the ledge of his control and fought to not tumble over.

Powerful pleasure rocked her body, turning it to jelly and making her glad she was already on her knees. She carried on taking it as sign he was getting pleasure.

Alternating between licking his length and sucking him into her mouth, she worked him.

His fingers tangled in her hair and slowly, he bopped her head up and down, controlling her movements, letting her know what pace he preferred. She'd always been a fast learner. Soon, she worked at his pace. His grunts got louder and quicker. She tried to increase the rhythm. But he pulled her off him and up.

"Did I do something wrong?" she asked, not hiding the disappointment in her voice.

"No, you didn't. You are wonderful."

He tugged her in and gave her a hot, hard kiss.

"But when I come, I want to feel your walls contracting all around me as you scream my name."

Body clenching at the imagery, she smiled. He shut off the faucet and reached for the large white bath towels hanging on the railing. He fluffed one over her body before wrapping her up in it. Then he flung one around his waist and pulled a canvas bag from the closet which he stuffed the wet clothes into it.

"I'm going to call the concierge to pick this up," he said. "Make yourself comfortable. I won't be long."

He slipped on a pair of shorts and disappeared out of the room. She stared at her reflection in the mirror. Her stomach rumbled in hunger pangs. She hadn't really eaten much at Ebony's house. And it seemed having sex made her hungry. She needed to find some food.

Since her own clothes were out of commission for the time being, she walked into Mark's closet in search of something to wear. She took a white shirt from his wardrobe and slipped it on. It turned out long enough to cover her bum and stopped mid-thigh.

With a quick glance in the mirror to fluff her hair, she headed out in search of the kitchen. The lights had come on in the hallway and she noticed the kitchen at the end of the hall opposite to the living room. She found the switch on the wall and turned on the light.

The kitchen looked sleek and modern, aluminium and white surfaces. In the middle of the room stood a centre-unit with five cooking hobs as well as a breakfast table with two stools. A huge, double-door, walk-in fridge-freezer stood at the end.

She opened it, surprised to find the fridge section stocked with fresh vegetables and fruits. A few items in plastic containers looked like tomato sauce or soup. She pulled out the carton of mango juice and went in search of a drinking glass in the cupboard closest to her. In it, she found spices and seasonings.

She carried on searching until she found the unit with the cups and plates. She took a glass out and poured a drink. While she was taking a sip, she heard a door closing. A few seconds later, Mark appeared at the kitchen door.

He whistled as he stared out her. "You look edible in my shirt. I like it."

"Look who's talking, walking around in nothing but a pair of shorts. A girl could get used to seeing all that masculinity on display."

He chuckled as he strode towards her with a predatory glint in his eyes. "I think we have some things to finish up."

"Yeah, about that. I need some food first. I'm hungry."

"Of course. Food. I can do that." He strode over to the fridge.

"You don't have to worry about cooking," she said, remembering that he didn't cook. "I saw some yoghurt in the fridge. I can have some of that."

"How about I make you an omelette?" He started taking items out of the fridge—eggs, cheese, and ham.

"Are you sure?" She frowned. "There's some tomato sauce in there. I can boil some rice."

"No. I want to make something fresh for you."

"Why?" She was even more baffled because he told her previously he never cooked himself and had a cook. She assumed the cook had gone home for the day.

"Because I want to cook for you, sweetheart." He caressed her cheek with the back of his hand. "I want to pamper you."

He leaned over and pressed a kiss to her lips. Her heart tightened and tears stung the back of her eyes. How could she not fall in love with him if he did things like that? Something she couldn't afford.

"Nobody has ever done that for me. I could get used to it."

"That's the idea. Sit." He pulled up the tall stool for her and she climbed on it.

He went about preparing the food. To her surprise, he moved around the kitchen like someone used to preparing and cooking food, at odds with the image she had of him.

He took a gleaming pan from the brushed steel rack hanging over the central unit and lit a gas hob. Then he plucked fresh herbs from the selections in a clear display vase. Even the ease with which he chopped up the ingredients spoke of expertise.

"I thought you said you couldn't cook."

"I told you I had a chef. I never said I couldn't cook." He raised his brows.

He had her there. She'd made assumptions about him based on the wrong things. "Oh."

He dished out two plates of cheese and ham omelette served with a side of lettuce salad and placed one in front of her before pulling up another stool beside her.

"Would you like some wine, madam?" He presented her with a bottle of South African Stellenbosch *Chenin Blanc*.

Her eyes widened. That was an expensive bottle of wine for just a plate of omelette. But she nodded. He opened the bottle and poured out the wine into two glasses before he sat down.

"Cheers." They clicked glasses and started eating.

"This is lovely," she said after taking a bite. "You can cook for me any day."

"You can visit me any day," he replied.

They ate in silence for a while.

"I'm curious as to the reason you didn't take a lover for so long," he finally asked.

His directness unsettled her sometimes. She welcomed his openness and honesty when it came to revealing things about him. But when he turned the focus on her, she became out of sorts. Her cheeks heated and she glared at him.

"How do you know it was a long time? I could've been with someone else last week."

"I doubt it. You were so tight; I'd wager a lot of money you haven't been with a man in years, a long time before we met."

"Yeah, you're right."

"Why, though? I'm sure it's not for lack of attention."

She shrugged. "Casual sex never appealed to me before and I hadn't met a man I wanted to give my body to in a long time. The available men are either too intimidated by my ambition, or want me to give up everything to become their wife. The only ones who seem to want me for me are married, and there's no way I'm touching another woman's husband. That's a no-go area for me."

"Well, it's all good news for me." He flashed a set of white teeth like a Cheshire cat.

"As long as you're not trying to chain me to the kitchen sink as your wife and you can handle the fact that one day, I might be taking over your business." She winked back at him playfully.

"Oh, you can try, sweetheart." He raised his glass. "Here's to getting what we want."

CHAPTER SEVEN

The day after a night of raunchy sex, delicious soreness in her body bore witness. The alarm on her phone woke her at five o'clock the following morning. She rose to find Mark already in the bathroom and they finally put his theory of shower sex to practice.

Her clothes had been cleaned, dried, and ironed, ready for her in his room when she came out of the shower. Even the buttons that had popped had been sown back into to the silk. She dressed without her undies. Another first.

Outfitted in his trademark pinstripe suit—a grey one today—and looking as commanding and sexy as always, Mark's comment of "knowing you left my house commando is going to keep me distracted for the rest of the day," bolstered her confidence. Perhaps she could play the sex kitten for Mark. Only Mark.

She stared at her reflection in the mirror in his closet, tugging at the straggly strands of her wet hair. Her underwear-less bum could easily be hidden beneath her knee-length linen skirt, but her messy head would be obvious to anyone who saw her. She couldn't afford to have people at work wondering why she wasn't looking her trademark sophisticated self, with no wish to be the topic of office gossip.

"What am I going to do about my hair?" she directed in dismay at Mark, busy knotting his navy blue tie. She would have to go home to get it sorted and that would mean being late for work. On a Monday! Not a good start to the week.

"Come with me." He took her hand.

She slipped her feet into her stilettos and followed him out of his room and down the corridor to another room, her heels tapping on the hard flooring. She loved this tactile Mark, always ready to touch her skin without prompting. He'd been this way at the beach and even the night in Johannesburg.

Warm and strong, his hands conveyed safety. Security. Was it just her mind playing tricks, conjuring illusions? Surely, she didn't need the safety of a man. She was secure in her own self.

"Here you go," he said when he pushed open the door.

Light and feminine, pink pastels and frilly fabrics decorated the large room.

"Whose room is this?"

The words left her mouth before she could curb them. Did one night with Mark give her possession of him? Could she now enquire as to whatever went on in his home as if she had claim over him? He didn't have a sister. And he'd told her his cook who doubled as a housekeeper was a man. Did he use to live with an ex?

She gave him a quick side glance, not budging as he tugged her to enter the room. She didn't want to step into a space that had been used by one of his exes. He seemed to see the tumult of emotions in her eyes as he smiled and squeezed her hand gently.

"It's Tari's old room."

He said that confidently, as if he was expecting her to know who the person was

"Who?" She frowned, her stomach knotting tightly with unease.

"You should know Tari, my baby cousin. She was a bridesmaid at Felix's wedding."

A brief image from the wedding of a light-skinned girl with a pretty face appeared in her mind.

"Oh, her." Faith glanced around the room. "She lives here?"

"No. She was staying here when she was at Law School because it was close." He lowered his voice conspiratorially, as if conveying a great secret.

Relief whooshed out of her body. She wasn't sure what she'd been expecting to hear.

"Truth is, she was a bit of a wild child and her parents wanted me to keep an eye on her."

His smile added just the killer charm. Her insides melted.

"Anyway, she's doing her Youth Service, so the room is empty."

"Okay," she replied, finally stepping into the room when he tugged her again.

"Check one of the drawers," he said, pointing in the direction of the small oak dresser with a gilded mirror on top. "I know she left a few things she didn't need and that girl had several blow driers. So there should be one someplace. I'll be in the kitchen making coffee."

Mark left her to it. She searched the dresser table drawers and found what she was looking for in the bottom right hand one, then she took out a small petroleum jelly jar from her bag. She never went anywhere without it. It came in handy both as a lip balm and hand cream.

A little dab with her fingers on her short-cropped hair and she blow-dried it into the style it'd been cut. Her reflection in the mirror confirmed she appeared ready for the day. No one would know she hadn't slept in her own house. Unless they'd seen her yesterday at the Christening wearing the same clothes. But that was highly unlikely, she hoped.

In the kitchen, Mark was pouring black coffee from the machine into two bone china cups. He'd set a place for her at the breakfast bar with a stool next to his, just like the previous night. He looked so comfortable playing the doting lover.

Did he do this same routine with all the other women he slept with, on the morning after? Her stomach tightened with nausea, the idea that she was just going to be another notch on his bed sickening her. She gritted her teeth and pushed the thought to the back of her mind.

Sex. This was all about sex. Nothing more. She needed to keep that at the front of her mind and stop forming any attachment to Mark. She needed to get away from him.

"I'm going to head off," she said in a casual voice to hide her apprehension as she stood at the threshold, knowing that if she walked into the kitchen, she would be pulled into the gravitational orbit that oozed around Mark. She hadn't been able to keep her hands off him in the shower this morning. And seeing him standing in his kitchen reawakened her arousal.

No need carrying on with this charade. They were not living in domesticated bliss, an option not open to her. She couldn't give another man license to ride roughshod over her mind. The one man who should've protected her—her father—only wanted her on his own terms. She couldn't be an individual free to make her own choices. She wouldn't allow another man to do that to her again. Mark only wanted sex. This was fine with her, for as long as she wanted it.

He turned around, a smile on his face.

"Not yet. Come and have some breakfast. I've got granola, fruit, and yoghurt." He gave an exaggerated sweeping wave at the table like a waiter.

She fought the smile that threatened to sneak out. She really couldn't let him charm her so easily.

"I'm not really a breakfast person," she said, hoping that would be the end of it.

"Breakfast is the most important meal of the day," he countered.

She should've known he would have a comeback.

"It's okay. I'll have a coffee and fruit when I get to the office. There are things I need to do before the working day starts." She tapped her forefinger on the face of her wristwatch.

He flicked his arm up and glanced at his gold watch then strode across the slate tiles in her direction. "I promise you, we'll be out of here by six thirty. Do we have a deal?"

She looked up into his midnight eyes. They sparkled, a smile playing on his lips. But she still knew he wouldn't back down until he got what he wanted.

Perhaps if she agreed, she could get out of there sooner. She took a deep breath. "Okay. Breakfast, then."

He held onto her hand as if he still expected her to bolt as they walked over to the stools. Seeing the food all laid out made her mouth water. She settled for some grapefruit and then ate a little cereal with yoghurt.

"What spooked you?" he asked her as he raised a spoon laden with granola and banana slices to his lips.

Her gaze lingered on his sensuous lips and she remembered how those same lips had sucked her breasts in the shower this morning, not to talk about all the other places on her body he'd licked and nipped last night. On her sex, his mouth had been like a suction cup, causing havoc and eliciting a few screams of pleasure from her. Her orgasms had come one after the other like the reputed London buses.

After five years of no orgasm, she'd had a series and had lost count after the fifth one. Her nipples tightened in remembrance and wetness slicked the junction of her thighs.

"Faith?"

His amused voice drew her attention and she shook her head to clear the haze of lust. She really had to get a grip. She turned her gaze to her bowl of cereal. Safer than staring at Mark.

"Sorry," she mumbled to hide her embarrassment.

"No need to be." His amusement still rang evident in his voice. "I wanted to know why you were ready to run again."

"Run?" She still didn't get him, and it seemed she was incapable of responding with more than one word at a time. *Somebody slap me now.*

"Something happened between when I left you in Tari's room to when you came into the kitchen. You...we...were having a good morning until then."

What the—! Could she not hide anything from this man? Obviously not. She lowered her hands to her lap and clenched them in frustration.

"How do you know that?" Her irritation slipped through her voice.

He stared at her for a moment, as if reading her some more. She lifted her brow in an 'answer-me' look.

"You had that same look in your eyes the night I was in your kitchen," he finally replied. "It's a mix of determination and fright. Every time I see it, I know something's happened in that brain of yours—" he touched her forehead with the pad of his forefinger, "—and you're about to bolt on me."

"Remind me never to play poker with you," she said in a sarcastic voice.

He shrugged. "Reading people is part of the reason I've been very successful. I can usually anticipate my opponents' actions before they are carried out and they never see mine coming." His grin gleamed full of white teeth, like a shark's. "So, tell me, what spooked you?"

"You did," she said, glad to see the smirk on his face disappear.

"Me? What did I do?" He drank the rest of his coffee.

"All of this." She waved her hands to encompass everything laid out on the table.

The gobsmacked expression on his face would've been comedic if she wasn't being serious.

"Walking in here to find you busy sorting out breakfast scared the hell out of me," she said honestly, glad to get it out in the open. The sooner they clarified their positions, the better for both of them.

"You don't like it?" He frowned, his disappointment obvious as he held her gaze.

For a moment, she thought she saw a shadow of hurt behind the glaze of his eyes. Her heart clenched. There it was. She didn't want to hurt him. But better she said it now rather than later.

"No," she replied quickly, not wanting him to misinterpret her words. "I like it. A lot."

"So what's the problem?" He still frowned.

"That's the problem. I shouldn't like it. I shouldn't care about it. After all, we're just having fun here, right? It's just sex—"

"Great sex," he interrupted.

"Good sex." She winked. "It's still just a casual thing, nonetheless. I was going to wake up, get dressed, and then head off to work and get on with my week." She paused, hand braced on the edge of the table. "And then you do this. This says it's more. This is domesticated in a we-have-a-future-together kind of way. And it's just not going to happen."

"So let me get this straight," he said, standing up to put his bowl and hers in the dishwasher. "Instead of kicking you out of my bed—"

"Correction. You can never kick me out. I'll be the one walking out when I've had my fill of you," she retorted, crossing her arms over her chest in a defensive stance as she bristled.

His eyes hardened into marbles as he leaned against the counter. His pose appeared casual but she wasn't fooled. She'd riled him.

"Right. So instead of letting you *sneak* out of my bed and my apartment like what we did was something to be ashamed of, I get up and pamper you with breakfast so that we can enjoy a little bit more time together before life gets in the way, and you don't like it."

The dangerous coldness to his voice should've rattled her. In fact, it did. But if this was a battle with Mark, she couldn't show any fear. She shrugged nonchalantly.

"Damn it, Faith. Would you rather I fuck you and send you home with money for the taxi fare? Is that the kind of relationship you want?"

His grip on the counter showed taut knuckles, his jaw clenched tight.

"You know damn well I don't need your taxi fare."

His insult stung. She didn't need his or any other man's money. Snatching her bag from where she'd left it on the table, she walked towards the door, her emotions churning. She needed to get out of there before she said something she would regret.

His fingers wrapped around her arm. She stopped walking but didn't turn around. Her heart pounded loudly in her ears. She heard the long whoosh of his breath before he walked around to face her. She looked up at his face but couldn't read his expression on the blank battle face she'd seen him wear on many newspaper pages.

"What do you want from me?"

His voice came out hoarse, telling her he wasn't as composed as he appeared.

"I want—" she squeaked and sucked in a deep breath to clear her head and voice before speaking more calmly. She tugged her arm and he let her go, and she wrapped them around her ribcage to hide her body's trembling.

"I don't want you to treat me like this is special when it's not," she said in a quiet voice, glad that she didn't sound as upset as she truly was.

"How do you know what we have is not special?" he asked, his hands crossed over his chest.

"Really?" She stared him down, meeting his gaze and showing no fear. "This is just sex, Mark. It might feel special—" she curled her fingers in air quotes, "—because it took us over a year to get here. But we don't have a future together. We're not Ebony and Felix."

He heaved a sigh and let his hands fall to his sides.

"I don't know what the future holds. Can we not just be in a relationship together, enjoying the here and now without worrying about the future?"

"I don't know if I can, Mark," she said with a hint of resignation in her voice. "I'm a planner. I can't get out of bed without having the whole day mapped out with back-up plans, too. I need to know what I'm doing... What we are doing."

"I can't plan what's going to happen with us," Mark said while raking his hand over his head in a frustrated gesture. "I've only just managed to get you here. All I know is that I want to be with you. I can't tell you how long we will last or when it will end."

"Perhaps not," she said in agreement. "But we will know when it's over, won't we? We're mature enough to be able to end it amicably, without drama, right?"

"Right," he said, and she noticed his jaw had clenched. He didn't seem to be one hundred percent convinced. "We can end it without drama when the time is right."

"Right. That's a plan I can live with." She nodded although the thought that they would break up one day didn't seem to agree with her heart, which clenched sadly.

"So can you let go and enjoy our time together, no matter how spontaneous it gets?" He closed in on her, his spicy scent and heat surrounding her body.

"I can." She nodded and swallowed as her body's awareness of his closeness ramped up.

"And will you let me pamper you, however I see fit?" Mischief had returned in his eyes.

She smiled. She liked his pampering.

"Yes," she managed to say in a breathless voice.

"Good." His fingers gripped her nape and his mouth descended on hers, sealing their agreement in a hot, bruising kiss.

A dull thud confirmed that her bag had slipped off her hand and dropped on the floor. She forgot where she needed to be and where she was. Her whole focus became Mark. Here and now. She stretched her hands upward, parting the lapels of his suit to find the soft cotton of his shirt beneath. A groan rang in her ears. Had it been from her or him?

A loud beeping made him lift his head. He inhaled a long breath and closed his eyes briefly. Then he reached into his suit pocket and withdrew his phone.

"Life has intruded," he said. "Time to go conquer the world."

He winked at her and picked her bag from the floor before handing it to her. With his hand on the small of her back, he led her out of the apartment. They took the lift in silence down to the lobby.

Outside, a black Mercedes Executive mini-limousine waited, the uniformed chauffeur holding the door open. She slid in. The inside smelled of leather and luxury. Mark spoke to the man briefly before joining her in the car.

She checked her phone for messages and glanced at the time. Six-thirty.

Lesson number four—Mark kept his word.

CHAPTER EIGHT

"I'm taking you away for the weekend," Mark breathed against satin smooth skin as he kissed a slow path up Faith's leg. "Pack a small bag."

Below him, Faith anchored herself onto her elbows and lifted her upper body, her left brow quirked up. "Where...? Why?"

Questions. She always had them, spontaneity never being her thing, though she had relaxed a whole lot since they started dating. Since the morning after the first time they'd had sex and he'd persuaded her to let him pamper her as he pleased.

Holding down her legs, he swiped the back of her left knee with his tongue. A long, drawn-out moan filled the air. How he loved that sound. A cry of surrender. A sign of her capitulation, if only for a short while. And he'd wrung it out of her. At times like this, the urge to channel his inner Neanderthal and pound his chest grew.

Instead, he curled his lips in a triumphant smile and licked the other knee, eliciting another moan from her.

"Why? You refuse to be seen anywhere in Lagos with me. I can't take you out to dinner or to the theatre or movies. I can't take you to a party or to a club." His frustration crept into his words.

She held his gaze, her brown eyes swirling with emotions. Desire. Sadness. Remorse.

"Mark, I'm sorry." She closed her eyes and her sigh floated in the air.

He pulled himself up and ghosted his lips over hers. "Don't be. You made your concerns clear right from the start and I accepted those conditions."

True. He had accepted her terms, as frustrating as they were. He'd never had to hide a girlfriend in the past, not even as a teenager. His parents had always wanted their sons to be open about the kind of company they kept. He was permitted to introduce a girl to his mother. Although these days, he didn't take a girl to his parents' house. He changed them so often it wasn't even worth the effort.

Until Faith.

This weekend would be their official one-month anniversary. He didn't even want to closely examine the fact that he remembered the date they'd first had sex. Perhaps it was because it had taken him a year to persuade her to let him in. He didn't care.

Fact remained, they'd dated for four weeks, most of which had been spent either at his apartment or hers. They needed a change of scenery.

"I know," she whispered, her eyes still closed. "But I still feel guilty about depriving you from the things you enjoy doing. You can still do those things. Just take someone else."

Leaning back, he sat on his heels between her spread legs. Taken aback by her words, he crossed his arms over his chest. This was a first, as far as he was concerned. A woman giving him the permission to take another woman on an evening out. Did she really think so little about their relationship?

Something stabbed his chest. Why did the thought hurt? He shouldn't care, if she didn't. So he enjoyed her company. She brightened up his day like sunshine, tasted as sweet as honey, and smelled as soothing as lavender.

Still, she was just a woman. And women couldn't be trusted. This was just another lay. He would move on one day. *Focus on the here and now.*

His gaze trawled over Faith's body arched as if in offering to him. Beautiful. Lush lips, full ripe breasts, narrow waist, flared hips, fleshy thighs. His very own heaven.

"Mark?"

He stared at her face puckered in a frown. And it hit him. As much as he wanted to delve in and continue as if her statement didn't bother him, he couldn't second-guess himself. Not for her. Not for any woman.

"Did you mean it?"

"What?" Her frown deepened.

"That I could take another woman to dinner or the movies."

Her eyes flicked to the left and downwards, her lower lip pulled into the corner. "Well, it's only to make sure you still do the things you enjoy. I mean, it's not as if we're married."

Lips pursed, he nodded. And then he uncrossed his arms and lowered them back onto her thighs, his grip a little firmer than before.

"Thank you for being so magnanimous." He yanked her thighs further apart, pushing her ankles back until her sex was bared to him, glistening, swollen, and trembling, waiting for his attention. He couldn't shake the anger simmering in his veins. His mother had been willing to share a man with another woman. To *be* the other woman.

What was it with women, anyway? Then they'd complain because a man didn't want to commit more than just the occasional booty call.

"Hold on to your ankles."

"Mark?"

"Do it, sweetheart. I'll make it worth your while." He winked at her.

She gave a nervous smile and grabbed onto her ankles. Good she complied, but she was right to be nervous. Playing fair didn't always get you what you wanted. And he wanted something right now from her. Her total attention and honesty.

Parting her lower lips with his left fingers, he circled around her clit with his index finger but not touching it and then trailed a wet path down her slit to the crack of her bottom. She whimpered and canted her hips.

"As I was saying," he carried on as if they were just chatting and he wasn't torturing her with his ministrations. "It's generous of you to be willing to share me with another woman. But the thing is...I'm not that generous. I'm not willing to share you with anyone. I want to be the one sitting across from you in a restaurant or sitting next to you in the mezzanine of a theatre. I want to be the one to walk you to your door after our date and give you a kiss good night or good morning, whichever the case. Do you understand?"

"Yes." Her word came out hoarse, as if she was out of breath.

"Good." Leaning over, he blew air at her sex and her body trembled. "I'm glad you understand. So I'm going to ask you again. Do you really want me to—" he chose his words carefully "—escort other women on occasions?"

"No," she gasped.

A cocky smile curled his lips and satisfaction lightened his chest. He wasn't done yet.

"Tell me what you want, sweetheart, and I'll give it to you," he hummed against her slit, moisture coating his lips.

"I want to be the only woman in your life." She quivered. "Well, apart from your relatives and professional colleagues, of course."

"You *are* the only woman in my life."

"Promise?"

"On my life."

Her eyes gleamed but she fidgeted with the sheet.

"What is it?" he asked.

"I want something else, as well."

"Name it."

"Make me come. Please"

"With pleasure, sweetheart." Her openness deserved a reward.

Without ado, he delved back in using his mouth to lick, nip, and suck, savouring her flavour, while his fingers pumped into her tight wet channel until she was writhing and moaning, the gratifying sound bouncing off the matted walls of his bedroom. She clawed the silk sheets and sang her climax, her body trembling until he'd wrung out the multiple orgasm and her body slumped.

Sheathed in protection, he lined up with her entrance and thrust in. Heat clenched around him. Constricting, rippling, wet heat. Drenched him. Tugged him. He had no other option but to slide out and pound into her, his hips thumping her cushiony bottom.

Fire sparked to life in his veins. Any time he held still, she wriggled, nudging his body heat to fever pitch, driving his control to the edge. When he sucked on her fleshy breasts or tugged her nipples, her whimpers just drove him insane.

Soon, he was ready to ride the wave but he wanted her there with him. So he reached between their sweat-slicked bodies and pushed down on her button with his thumb. The ripples of her orgasm pulled his over the edge and he gripped her hips, arms bunched and head tilted back as he roared his release.

For seconds, he lay slumped above her, holding his body on his elbows so he didn't crush her as he caught his breath. Reclining and limp, she appeared sated. Replete.

His breath caught. Droopy lids lifted and smoky brown eyes stared up at him. Her lips curled in a slow smile. She reached up and wrapped her hands around his neck, pulling him down for a kiss.

"Thank you," she said when they pulled apart, panting.

"Why are you thanking me?" When his strength returned to his body, he slid out of her, holding onto the condom. Standing, he disposed of the latex.

He'd made her a promise that he would protect her from the risk of pregnancy and he needed to make sure he kept to his word. Her protection was *his* responsibility.

"For giving me what I wanted." Her smile looked coquettish.

"Sweetheart, giving you what you want is why I'm here." He settled back in the bed beside her.

"No one has ever said that to me before. You sound so sincere."

"I wouldn't say it unless I meant it." He pulled her into his arms and tucked the sheet around them. "When I was a teenager, my father taught me a phrase—a promise made is a promise kept. I've lived by those words since I became an adult."

He stroked hair away from her forehead and placed a kiss in the middle.

"Those are wise words to live by. I'll hold you to them."

"Please do," he whispered against her skin.

A few heartbeats later she asked, "So where are we going for this dirty weekend?"

"It's a secret."

"But I need to know so I can make travel arrangements, buy tickets, you know."

He lifted his head and eyed her. "No need to worry about it. This is my treat. It's all paid for. All you need to do is show up."

"Mark, you know I'm uncomfortable having you pay for everything." She turned her face away. "I really don't want it to seem I'm with you for what I can get out of you."

He'd never been with a woman reluctant to let him treat her. In fact, his exes were never shy about making requests for gifts or even treats, and he'd never turned any request down. Women needed pampering. And money bought the good things in life.

He tucked his knuckle under her chin and tugged until she faced him again.

"Faith, I know you are not with me for my money. But I'm a wealthy man and I can afford to pay for this trip."

"It's not just about—"

"Look, how about a compromise? Any treats or surprises I come up with, I pay for, and if you choose to treat us to any surprises of your own, you pay for them yourself. Sounds fair?"

She pouted before nodding.

"Good. So just pack a small bag. You will need comfortable walking shoes and perhaps a pair of hiking boots and an outdoor jacket."

Their trip out was uneventful. He'd arranged for a car to pick Faith up and drop her at the heliport in Victoria Island, close to his apartment. The helicopter ride took just ten minutes as opposed to the two hours it would have taken them to get from the Island to Ikeja on a Friday evening.

As they flew into the domestic airport by helicopter, they didn't need to go through the normal check-in channels and were fast-tracked through to the lounge. Luckily, they didn't have long to board the plane and settled next to each other. An hour's flight out to Calabar and then they took another helicopter ride out to their destination.

The Obudu Mountain Resort sparkled in the darkness, matching the huge grin on Faith's face as they arrived. Warmth spread through his body. Convincing her to come away for the weekend had been a good idea.

They were met at the helipad by the resort manager who greeted and ushered them to their villa. His security detail walked behind with their bags.

The wooden villa stood on stilts built into the mountain face and was filled with modern conveniences.

"This is a piece of heaven away from home," Faith said and kissed him when they were left alone again.

"Does that mean you're glad to be here?" He pulled her close.

"Absolutely."

The weekend passed blissfully for both of them with no worries of paparazzi or being recognised. Even his bodyguard kept a discreet distance while they were exploring. They took the cable car across the mountain, getting a breathtaking view of the lush green landscape high up in the Obudu Mountains. They strolled through the wildlife sanctuary, watched water cascade down crystal clear waterfalls.

On Saturday evening, they enjoyed dinner outdoors on the mountain restaurant and watched the sun set in the horizon.

"We're so high up I feel I can reach out and touch the sky."

"You probably can, if you stand on my shoulders." He winked at her.

"Oh, you." She giggled.

The soft, tinkly sound poured fuel on the flame that had been burning within him all day. He really wanted to get her indoors, but they needed food after all the activities they'd done that day.

"You know this is the first time I've had a holiday of sorts with anyone."

"But I thought you said you've been to London."

"Yeah, for studies and work. And yes, I took a two-week break a couple of years ago before I started working as Strategy Director, but then, I travelled on my own."

He frowned. "Are you saying you never went on holiday with your family when you were a child? Not even to your hometown?"

Every city-dwelling Nigerian child ventured to his or her hometown village at least once in their lifetime. As tradition, Nigerians were big on their ancestry and roots. Even he remembered holidays in Calabar, his father's hometown.

"Technically, Benin is my hometown. It's only thirty minutes from my father's house to the Brown family compound. So I guess in my head, I never really saw any visits there as a holiday. Not in the sense of getting away from it all."

"Oh, I see."

"What about you? Did you have family holidays as a child?"

"Yes, we did visit Calabar frequently when I was growing up. I enjoyed my time there."

"Ebony told me her family used to holiday with yours in London. When Alex was born, she was showing me some old photographs of her and Felix as children which her mum had in albums."

Mark leaned away and swallowed. His back stiffened and the urge to get up and walk away rose. He lowered his hands and gripped onto the arms of the chair, fighting his rising gloom.

Faith didn't know what she was doing by talking about the past. To her, it was but a harmless reference.

Yet, the old hurt rose inside and hunched his shoulders.

"Mark, what's wrong?"

"Nothing," he said in a stiff voice and rolled his shoulders.

"Tell me what's gone wrong. You look as if I've just killed your pet or done something terrible."

"It's okay. It doesn't matter."

"Well, it matters to me that something has upset you. *Mbok*."

"What did you just say?"

"*Mbok*. That's how to say 'please' in Efik, isn't it? Did I get it wrong?" She fiddled with her wristwatch as she frowned.

Joy grew within him and he let it curl his lips in a smile. "You got it right. I was just shocked to hear you speak Efik."

He reached across and pulled her hands up and brushed his lips against her knuckles.

"For that, you deserve an explanation." He stood. "Let go for a stroll and I'll explain."

Hand in hand, they walked at a gentle pace, watching the night settle in around them, their path lit by floor-level street lamps, the only sound that of chirping crickets.

He exhaled a sigh and tried to explain his previous jumbling emotions.

"I don't know if you know this already, but when I was born, my mother was not married to my father."

"I didn't know that," she said as she looked up at him, her eyes widened in surprise.

Many people who didn't know his family history would be surprised by the knowledge, too. This history formed a huge part of who he was, layered in pain and disappointment.

"Dad was married to Felix's mother and was having an affair with my mother. Don't get me wrong, he was a good father. Well, as good as he could be since I only saw him once a month. But he made sure we had everything I needed. I went to the best schools, had the most expensive toys. My mother even took me on holidays abroad."

He paused and swallowed.

"But you see, those you refer to, the family ones which Felix enjoyed in his formative years. I never had them. Because while Chief was my father, he was only an occasional dad. I'd be lucky to see him two weekends in a row. And we never travelled together. Not until we were all living together after Felix's mum passed away."

Faith squeezed his hand. "That must've been very tough on you."

"It was. At a point, I resented Felix. He had what I wanted. My father's attention." His mother's competitiveness hadn't helped, either. She'd resented that his father hadn't divorced his wife. And her resentment had seeped into him. He'd taken it out on Felix.

He heaved a heavy sigh and scrubbed a hand on his head.

"Fact remains, it wasn't Felix's fault. He was a victim of the situation as much as I was. But what the whole situation taught me was that if I ever have children, I would be in their lives one hundred percent of the time."

She stopped in front of him, stood on her tiptoes, and reached for his neck. Then she leaned in and kissed him. "I know you will make a great dad one day."

CHAPTER NINE

"I think we've finally got a means of getting rid of Petersen," Chief Essien said.

Mark, Felix, Tony, and Kola sat on the upholstered sofas in the Essien patriarch's den. The room rambled large enough to have a bank of four sofas on one end and a wall covered with bookshelves and a large desk at the other. Their father's sanctuary, where he entertained his guests and, on a Sunday like this, where they met up to discuss the Apex business dynasty outside of office hours.

Once a month on a Sunday afternoon, the Essien brothers got together at the family home in Ikoyi. Mark's mother had started the tradition when the two older boys had moved out of home and bought their own places. She'd wanted a means for them to come together outside of work. Truth was, Mark saw his brothers regularly, anyway.

He used to have weekly meetings with Felix when neither of them were travelling. But that had been before his brother's marriage to Ebony, and even less now since the arrival of baby Alex. His brother loved spending all his spare moments with his family.

Right now, Ebony and Alex were with his mother.

Faith should be with them, too.

His jaw tightened. The woman still refused to be seen anywhere with him and had turned down all his previous invitations to similar gatherings.

Anyway, the Sunday lunches being a strictly Essien affair, bringing her here would amount to declaring his intentions to his family. Was he ready for that? Perhaps it proved a good thing she refused to date him publicly. He didn't have to deal with the speculation from his entourage or the media.

"What do you mean?" Mark asked, his thoughts veering back to the matter being discussed.

"There's a rumour that Petersen is involved in insider trading," his father replied.

"In which case, the EFCC need to investigate his share trading activities," Mark said matter of factly.

"The downside of that is that we would have to expose EFCC to Apex," Felix said. "After the recent failed board coup and vote, it wouldn't be a good thing to put Apex PB under scrutiny."

"I don't want the EFCC anywhere near Apex," his father said. "This is where Kola comes in. I've asked him to investigate Petersen's financial activities."

"I've already set the ball rolling," Kola said. "I've got our best data forensics specialist on it. Whatever paper trail exists, he'll find it, whether it is physical or digital."

"Good," Chief Essien said. "In the meantime, there's an opportunity to strengthen our holdings. You remember Francis Okolo?"

"Sure. What about him?" Mark piped up.

"I met up with him at the Ikoyi Club yesterday. He informed me he will be retiring soon and is looking to handover to a new successor."

Mark sat up. Francis Okolo was the majority shareholder at City Investments Group. The same firm where Faith worked as Strategy Director. Did she know about this?

"Does that mean City is up for sale?" Felix asked the question on Mark's mind.

"Not openly. His retirement is not public knowledge yet, just a conversation among friends. But I know he will consider offers privately. This is where you come in, Mark."

"City has very big influence in the Oil and Gas sector," Mark said. "For years, we've been trying to get into the same market segment with little organic progress. Buying City would be a great development for Apex Investments."

"It would," Felix concurred as their father nodded.

"You want me to make Mr. Okolo an offer?" Mark asked just to be sure he knew where his father was headed.

"Put together a proposal. One he can't refuse," Chief Essien said. "Francis treats City as his baby and he would want to make sure that it is in good hands when he retires. He is big on continuity, but none of his children are interested in running the business apart from as investments. So we want to guarantee him that we will keep up the good work with minimal job losses through an acquisition. Of course, the fact that we've been friends for years should smooth the way."

"No problem," Mark said. "I'll find out as much as possible about City and work on a proposal before the weekend as I'm going to New York next week."

"Good. I want the bones of this fleshed out before your trip. I will call him and arrange a meeting for Friday. The lawyers can work on the details while you're away."

Mark nodded and pulled out his smart phone to punch in a note on his calendar. A notification pinged that he had a message.

His pulse jumped in anticipation. The ID confirmed the text came from Faith. Not a day went by without some form of communication between them. He swiped the screen and opened the message.

How's your day going?

The conversation around him had moved on to other, more domestic issues, so he excused himself. He needed to hear Faith's voice although she'd only left his apartment a few hours previously.

He strode outside into the gazebo and pressed the button to dial her number. She picked it at the first ring.

"Hello, handsome." Her velvety voice came through.

A smile curled his lips. It always did when she addressed him that way. "Hi, sweetheart. What are you doing?"

"Just chilling. I was trying to sort out my chores since I spent all of yesterday hanging out with you."

His smile got wider as he remembered all they'd done the previous day. A lot of it had been spent horizontal, even if not all in bed.

"I can't seem to think about anything else when I'm around you."

"Yeah, don't I just know it. Muscles I didn't know I had are still aching."

He chuckled. "Sex is a great workout, you know."

She laughed this time, the tinkling sound going right through to his groin. His granite need swelled and he groaned out loud.

"Do you know what the sound of your laughter does to me? I want you right now."

"Mark!" She giggled. "You had me more times than I can count yesterday."

"I'm just saying. You make me feel like a horny teenager, and I can't seem to get enough of you."

"You make me feel like a beautiful, desirable woman, and I love it when you touch me." Her silky voice dropped an octave, setting fire to his body.

"You are killing me," he growled and shut his eyes, imagining her bare, curvaceous body under his as he rode her, driving both of them to completion. "I'm going to need a very cold shower tonight."

"Perhaps you should come over, after all."

He opened his eyes. He found himself very tempted to hop into his sports car and race over to her house right now. His family wouldn't be happy if he cut short their Sunday ritual, though. They hadn't had dinner yet. He took a deep breath and common sense prevailed.

"But you said you had chores to do."

"It's all done now."

He let out a sigh. She'd complained of being sore and he didn't want to be selfish, as much as his body hated him for that choice. "I rode your body pretty hard yesterday, partly because I knew I wouldn't see you today. I think you should rest."

"Aww. Spoilsport," she said, but he heard the humour in her voice.

He laughed out loud and stopped when he spotted his mother walking towards the gazebo. "Listen, I've got to go."

"Okay, But call me later tonight. I think I'm in the mood for some phone sex." She giggled.

He suppressed a groan. "Oh, I'm going to get you for that."

"Promise?" she teased.

"Bye, sweetheart."

"Bye, handsome."

He tucked his phone back into his back pocket as he stood from the chair.

"Mum, is dinner ready yet?" he asked, wondering if that was why she'd sought him out.

"Yes. But I wanted to talk to you one-to-one first before we go in."

"It sounds serious. Is everything okay?" He waited for her to sit before he settled back in his chair.

"Of course. I just wanted to catch up with you. I don't see you so often these days. Is all well with you?"

"Sure, Mum. Everything is good. Business is great." He lifted his shoulders in a shrug.

She nodded. "That's good to know. Are you seeing someone?"

"What do you mean?"

"I mean, do you have a girlfriend?"

"Mum, what kind of question is that?"

"It's a simple question, my son." She smiled. "You either have a girlfriend or you don't. Knowing you, you are rarely between girlfriends."

"How do you know how often I have girlfriends?" Not as if he'd been bringing girls home since he moved out of the family home to go to University.

"You ask that as if your girlfriends are supposed to be secrets."

True. But Faith was a secret he hadn't shared with anyone except Felix. And Felix would never share a secret.

"Mum, what is this all about?"

"Look. The gossip magazines usually have pictures of you with one girl or the other. But for the past few months, I haven't seen anything, so I'm just wondering if there's someone."

He scratched the stubble on his jaw, contemplating whether to let his mother believe he had no girlfriend at the moment. But the idea of lying to her didn't sit well with him. So he settled for the partial truth.

"I'm seeing someone but it's just fun. Nothing serious."

"That's all right, then, because I invited Wumi Adekunle to join us for dinner. She's a really nice girl, from a nice family—"

"Hang on a minute, Mum. You invited Wumi...for me?"

"Yes, I know she likes you, and the two of you used to get along when you were younger."

"Mum, that was then. I mean, we are friends, but that's all there is."

"If you give her a chance, there could be more."

"I'm not looking for more. Wumi wants engagement rings and wedding bells. I'm not interested in that. I'm quite happy to just have fun at the moment."

"There's nothing wrong with wedding bells. Your brother, Felix, is married and he is happy. You can have the same."

Here we go again. His competitive mother in action. He'd thought they'd gone past this phase of comparing him with his older brother. Obviously not.

"I don't have to do what Felix does. Moreover, he loves Ebony. I don't love Wumi. Huge difference." He stood and paced to and from the gazebo. If he'd brought Faith here, he wouldn't have to be dealing with all this. But his mother spoke of wedding bells and he wasn't ready for that even with Faith.

"You can grow to love her. You just have to give her a chance. I'm sure the two of you can have fun, as you put it, to start with. Then, after a few months, you can start making plans for a future together."

"I can't believe we're having this conversation. You cannot pick my girlfriends for me."

"Wumi is not just girlfriend material; she is a potential wife." His mother leaned forward. "This is just going to be a family dinner with her around. Talk to her."

"All I'm going to do is talk. I can't promise you more than that."

He couldn't believe he was agreeing to this but sometimes, it just proved easier to agree with his mother than to argue with her. Moreover, Wumi knew the score. If she didn't, he would reiterate it. They could never get involved that way.

"It's good enough for me." His mother smiled and stood. "Come, let's go inside."

He heaved a sigh and followed her indoors.

Everyone had regrouped in the family room. Tony, Felix, and his father watched a football game on big, flat-screen TV hanging on the far wall, while Wumi bounced baby Alex on her lap as she chatted with Ebony.

"Hello, Wumi," he said when he entered the room.

She beamed him a smile, handed the baby to Ebony, and stood. "It's good to see you again, Mark."

Courtesy demanded that he give her the welcome double kisses on both cheeks. With his family looking on, he didn't want to be rude. So he strode across to her.

She was dark-skinned and tall, taller than Faith. But while Faith came across as a bundle of silky-smooth curves, Wumi appeared athletically slim. A member of the Ikoyi Running Club, she also played tennis regularly. To be fair, she was a pretty woman, and dressed in a brandy-coloured, long-sleeved draped v-neck designer dress and matching sequin-embellished T-strap high-heeled sandals, she knew it, too.

As he quickly brushed his lips against her skin and inhaled her musky fragrance, nothing stirred within him. Nada. *Ba kome. Ihe efu.* Not a spark.

A smile played on his lips as he remembered how the smell of Faith made him feel at home. Sunshine and lavender.

"Oh, no!"

The men behind him chorused and Mark turned to see what was happening on the TV. Another of their Sunday family rituals, watching Premier League football together.

"I can't believe he hit the bar again," Felix said and met Mark's gaze, his brow quirked in a 'what's going on?' query.

Mark shrugged and took a seat on the arm of a sofa away from where Wumi sat so he could watch the match. Nothing should interfere with this one ritual.

His mother stepped into the living room. "Dinner is ready. You can watch that game later."

Well, except for dinner, of course. Nothing messed with their food. Not even football. They all stood and filed out, heading to the formal dining room.

As they all sat down, he wished Faith sat next to him, instead of Wumi. Only one thought got him through the next hours—his upcoming telephone conversation with Faith.

Luckily, Wumi didn't stay long after dinner. He walked her to her Mercedes SLK200 roadster convertible. She'd received it as a birthday present last year from her family; he'd been there at the party.

Her father was a wealthy industrialist, and she had a great job as Assistant Finance Director at City Investments, Co. She lacked for nothing, and he could never accuse her of gold-digging.

But he'd never seen her as anything more than a friend. Even when they'd been teenagers and she'd played sports with the boys, he'd never thought about hitting second base with her, although they'd shared a kiss once.

She would make a good wife to some guy. Just not him.

"Would you like to get together sometime this week, Mark?"

Her soft words drew him out of his reverie.

"I've got a very heavy schedule this week. Perhaps another time."

"Okay, I'll hold you to that." She smiled gracefully. "I haven't seen you at tennis for a while. Will you be there on Saturday?"

Warmth crept up his cheeks. His Saturdays had been so taken over by Faith that he'd stopped hanging out with his friends. If only he could persuade Faith to come with him to the Ikoyi Club. She didn't have to play. She could just watch him while he played.

"Perhaps I'll be there this weekend," he said.

She leaned forward to kiss him and he turned his face so her lips brushed his cheek.

"See you soon, Mark." She lowered her body into the car seat.

He shut the door and straightened. "Bye."

He didn't stay long afterwards. Before he got into his car, he sent a text to Faith.

I'm heading home now. I'll call you when I get in. Wear something sexy.

CHAPTER TEN

"I'm sorry to have to change our weekend plan," Faith said into her phone.

She should've known that throwing down the gauntlet for Mark would only make him more determined and rise to the challenge. His persistence in pursuing her in the year since she'd met him at the conference in South Africa had proven his determination.

And even after that long night they spent together at his apartment, she'd thought his interest would've waned because he'd achieved what he wanted—racking up another notch on his bedpost.

They'd been seeing each other for the past six months, although not as frequently as the first few weeks. These days, making time had become trickier, especially since she still didn't want anyone else to find out. Only Ebony and Felix knew about them.

"So you mean I'm not going to see you this weekend?"

Mark didn't sound altogether pleased about that, although his tone came across as teasing.

Faith held her phone to her ear as she waited in the queue to check into her flight to Benin.

"I won't be back until Sunday," she said in a low voice but tried to keep it loud enough to be heard over all the other people in the busy domestic flights terminal.

"But I'm on a flight to New York on Sunday, so I probably won't see you then. I've got an important meeting on Monday with some investors that I can't miss."

"Oh." Disappointment curdled her stomach. She hadn't realised he would be going away for the week. "How long are you away for?"

"I'll probably be gone a week. But I'll try and be back as soon as my business is concluded."

Strange. Since they'd started their affair, they'd seen each other regularly and for periods of no more than three days apart at a time. Even with Mark travelling frequently, he only stayed away two or three days in one go.

She wanted to ask him about the nature of his trip. But they'd agreed earlier on to keep their business dealings separate from their relationship. They never discussed work, at least not when it had something to do with their businesses. They discussed generic industry matters but nothing that could be construed as corporate operations.

"Do I take it you're going to miss me, then?"

"Perhaps." She shrugged though he couldn't see her. In her heart, she knew she would miss him. She'd been hoping to see him as soon as she returned from Benin, knowing she would need his brand of pampering. Visiting her parents always proved a stressful event.

"Well, I'm going to miss you," he said in a husky voice that had her insides melting. "I wish you could come with me."

"Yeah, right. What am I going to do with myself while you attend meetings all day?"

"It's New York, sweetheart. You can always shop. Women love that, right?"

She smiled. "Some retail therapy *would* be good."

But something about going with Mark and playing his mistress while he worked didn't quite sit well with her.

"Anyway, I have loads to do over here. So maybe next time."

"Sure. Next time."

She moved to the front of the queue. "Mark, I'm going to have to call you back. I need to check in."

"Sure. I'll give you fifteen minutes and I'll call you back," he said and hung up.

Getting through check in didn't take too long since she only had the carry-on luggage. On the other side, she walked to the lounge and found a space to sit that wasn't already crowded.

It certainly beat doing the three hour drive from Lagos to Benin, on a good day. A few years ago she used to take the luxury coaches to Benin and back. When she bought her first car, she drove the distance. These days, she could afford the air fare, so she preferred taking the one hour flight.

True to his word, Mark called her back.

"So tell me why you're making an unplanned trip to Benin?" he asked as soon as she'd picked up.

Mark was one of the most direct men she'd ever known. He never sugar-coated anything.

"I told you already, my brother called to tell me that my mum was not feeling well," she replied.

"But you mentioned she wasn't in hospital. So what exactly is wrong with her?"

"I don't really know. It could be malaria, for all I know. I've already sent money for her to see a doctor. But I still want to go and see her. I haven't visited them for a few months." She travelled home less often these days.

"I hope it's nothing serious and she gets better before you get there."

"Thank you."

"And if it is something serious, let me know as soon as you find out. If she needs to come to a hospital in Lagos, I know some very good doctors that will take care of her."

A fist squeezed her heart and tears stung her eyes. Mark's compassion in wanting her mother to get well was one thing. But his generosity in going out of his way to take care of a woman who wasn't his responsibility touched her in a place no other person had reached in a very long time.

The words choked in her throat as she dug for tissue in her bag to dab at her eyes so she didn't smear her mascara all over her face and look like a panda.

"You don't have to do that," she said in a choked voice, considering she hadn't told him much about her family—she'd always avoided talking about them whenever he'd asked, and he'd never pressed her for more, of which she was grateful.

"But I want to. Seriously, let me know if there's anything I can do as soon as you get there, so I can get the ball rolling before I head off to New York tomorrow."

"Okay. I will. Thank you, but I hope it'll be something minor."

"I hope it's nothing serious, too."

"So, what are you going to do with yourself while I'm gone all weekend?" she asked in a teasing tone to change the subject from her family. Still shaky grounds for her, that topic.

"I don't know. Isn't it interesting that since we started hanging out regularly over the weekend, nothing else seems to matter but just being with you?"

She smiled. He really did know how to butter up her ego.

"I guess I'm just going to have an even longer workout at the gym to use up all this energy that I've been piling up all week. It's going to be one long weekend."

She laughed out loud and lowered her voice when people stared at her.

"Perhaps I should call Wumi and find out if she's available for a game of tennis."

"Wumi?" Alarm bells went off in her head. "Why do you want to play tennis with her?"

"We used to play tennis regularly on Saturdays with some other friends. That was before you." He said it as if there was nothing wrong with that. "She's probably got other playing partners, anyway, so she won't be available. But you don't mind, do you? It's just tennis."

She wanted to scream, 'hell, no!' But that would have been so jealously childish. He'd promised her there was nothing going on between him and Wumi, and in the time they'd been seeing each other, she'd had no reason to think there was. All his spare time had been spent with her. So why should she have a problem with him playing tennis with Wumi?

But the image of Wumi hanging on his arm throughout that party in Johannesburg stayed in her head. Wumi still wanted Mark and would seize any opportunity to be with him. But Faith needed to trust Mark. He wouldn't cheat on her with the woman.

"Of course, you can play tennis with Wumi," she said and tried not to choke on her own words. It took all she had to keep a casual tone. "It's just tennis, and I don't want it to seem like I'm keeping you away from your friends."

He laughed. "They already think that you keep me away from them. Apart from the occasional event that I attend and my catch up time with my family, the only other person outside business I spend time with is you."

"What? You've told your friends about me?" Blood drained from her head as she panicked. "You promised to keep it a secret," she nearly shouted at him.

"Of course not," he countered. "I promised you I wouldn't tell anyone about us. I mean, Felix and Ebony already know. But I would never betray you like that."

She heaved a sigh of relief. "Sorry. For one horrid moment, my imagination ran away with me."

"I still don't understand why we need to sneak around like school children. We are two consenting adults and should be able to do whatever we want."

She understood his frustration but he knew that their secret getting out would be a deal breaker for her.

"I told you I don't want it affecting my professional life. I really don't want to rehash this, Mark."

He heaved a frustrated sigh. "Oh, well. I guess I'm just irritated I won't see you for a few days, perhaps for over a week."

Her flight was called on the tannoy, interrupting their conversation.

"If it helps, I will miss you," she said and shook her head. When did she become so soppy?

"It helps."

She could hear the smile in his voice. "I've got to board my flight now. I'll call you when I get there."

"So, do I get a kiss?"

His sign-off signature whenever they spoke on the phone. While she didn't mind doing it in the privacy of her home, she'd rather not blow a kiss in a very public venue like an airport.

"Mark, I'm at an airport lounge," she whispered.

"I know, but I still want my kiss."

She glanced around the room. People milled around, preparing to board their flights.

"Faith Brown, I want my kiss, otherwise, I'm boarding the next flight out to Benin to come and get it in person."

She gasped. "You wouldn't!"

"You know better than to dare me," he replied with what sounded like a smirk.

She *did* know better. After all, he was the same man who had kissed her at the party in Johannesburg, the first night they'd met! He had no problems with public displays or taking what he wanted. And the last thing she wanted was him turning up in Benin. She wasn't ready for the fallout that would follow such an event.

"Okay. Okay." She turned her back on the crowd and stepped away, cupping her hand around the mouthpiece of the phone. "Muah!"

"Muah to you, too, sweetheart," he said in a husky voice. "Have a safe flight."

Their conversation stayed with her as she boarded the flight and even after the plane had levelled out in the sky. The sense of euphoria remained until the pilot announced they would be landing shortly. Knots of anxiety then tied her stomach.

As they disembarked, she caught herself twisting her watch around. She always did that when anxious. She huffed out an annoyed breath that, at the age of twenty-nine and as successful as she was professionally, she still got nervous about seeing her parents.

She blanked her mind, refusing to think about it, and focused instead on finding a taxi to take her to her parents' house. As the car drove through the city, she mused about how the place hadn't changed much from the one she grew up in, another indicator of the things to come.

Compared to the twenty-four-seven bustle of Lagos, Benin provided a more laid-back approach. Leafy and sedate, the city's huge draw was its cultural heritage as the heart of the ancient Benin Empire, a Kingdom that existed between 1440 and 1897. Some people confused it with the country of Benin formerly known as Dahomey.

"*Eten*, Faith," Odion shouted from the gate, his excitement apparent. He rushed to give her a hug and take her travel bag. "Welcome."

At least, her kid brother was always pleased to see her.

"Thank you, Odion." She squeezed his lanky body briefly. "How are you?"

"I'm very well. It's so wonderful you came. I was going to call you. I just went out to buy some credit for my phone."

"Oh, what happened? Is Mama worse?"

"No. Nothing like that. My results came. I got a place to study History at the University of Benin."

"That is wonderful. Congratulations. Where is Mama?"

"She's inside with Papa."

Faith followed her brother as he carried her bag inside and they exchanged more news about his university placement.

Inside, her father sat on his designated dark-red upholstered armchair watching a programme on the TV. In this house, the television almost stayed on at all times except during a power outage. Pictures of her father and mother hung on the peach-coloured walls.

"Good morning, Papa."

"What are you doing here?" he asked from his chair as he looked her up and down like something that had just crawled in from the gutter. Neither his expression nor his tone of voice sounded welcoming.

Her stomach churned and she gritted her teeth. "I came to see Mama. I heard she was unwell."

He grunted and waved her on. Faith swallowed the lump in her throat and fought back tears as she walked into the corridor leading to the back of the house.

"Is Mama in her room?" she asked Odion once they were away from the prying eyes of their father.

"Is that my daughter's voice I can hear?" Her mother's voice came from the kitchen.

"Yes, it's me, Mama."

Her mother poked her head out of the kitchen door just as Faith arrived at the entrance.

"What a pleasant surprise." Her mother hugged her before looking her over like she always did to check that she was fine. "Is everything alright?"

"Everything is fine with me, Ma. I should be asking you how you are doing. Odion called me yesterday and told me you haven't been well for a few days.

"My dear, I've been unwell for a while, but it comes and goes." Her mother pulled up a chair for her to sit but Faith waved her hand away and indicated for her to sit, instead.

"What exactly is wrong?" She scrunched her face up in worry, her initial agitation about her father now replaced with worry for her mother.

"I get aches all over my body but the painkillers don't seem to help."

"How long has this been going on?"

"It's been a few weeks." Her mother shrugged.

"A few weeks? Why did nobody tell me?" She glanced accusingly at Odion.

"I only found out a few days ago, I swear," he protested. "You know how good Mama is at hiding things."

Faith turned back to her mother. "Why didn't you tell anybody? What did the doctor say?"

"At first, I thought it was just malaria and have been taking tablets. But the aches didn't go away. So I went to see the doctor on Friday. They took blood for tests. They will let me know next week."

"Didn't they want to keep you in for observations or something?"

"Ah, I can't stay in the hospital all weekend. I can't just leave your father and brother here by themselves. Who will take care of them?"

"Mama! You are the one who should be taken care of. Odion and Papa are not babies. They should be able to take care of themselves."

Faith paced up and down in the kitchen as she got more and more agitated. This was always the case in this house. Her mother slaved like a workhorse to take care of the household. From the time she'd been a child, it had always been that way.

As a teenager, she'd hated to see her mother struggle so much. When she'd found out her father had a similar future in store for her, she'd rebelled. She'd wanted to do other things instead of being treated like a doormat by a husband and children.

She'd left home at the first opportunity and refused to regret it. The consequence had been her father practically disowning her and banning her from coming back there. But she refused to stay away. She loved her mother and brother too much.

"Listen, Mum, how about you come to Lagos with me for a few days?"

Her mother's eyes widened and it looked like she was going to object. Faith carried on.

"Just for a few days. I'm sure whatever is wrong with you won't be helped by you being constantly on your feet. In Lagos, you will get to relax and be pampered. You won't have to lift a finger. And I can book you in to see a very good doctor friend of mine. Eh, please, Mama. For me." She squatted in front of her mother.

The older woman beamed a loving smile on her as she took her hands into her warm grasp.

"All right. I will go to Lagos with you. But we have to speak to your father about it."

Dread curled in Faith's stomach like a worm. Not good.

"I'll go and speak to him now," she said bravely and tried to stand up.

"No." Her mother held her hand. "Wait until later. I will talk to him first."

Faith nodded, somewhat relieved that she didn't have to face down her father who'd always said 'no' whenever Odion or her mother had wanted to come visit her in Lagos. She being the family outcast, anyone who disobeyed him and came to see her would be cast out themselves.

In all her years, her parent had never blatantly disobeyed her father, although there'd been times when she'd walked the line in secret.

So Faith hoped her mother could persuade her father to let her go to Lagos, at least for a week.

"Odion, go and put your sister's bag in my room."

"No, Mama. You know Papa won't let me spend the night here. I will stay at the hotel."

Another consequence of being the family outcast. She couldn't spend the night in the house. Her father proved very unforgiving. The only way around it would be to grovel to him and beg to be let back in.

But Faith wasn't going there.

Her mother sighed. "I wish you and your father will stopping this constant fighting. You are both so alike in your stubbornness."

"Mama, I'm not even going to talk about that right now." Faith went over to the kitchen counter. "What was it you were preparing? Let me help you do it."

CHAPTER ELEVEN

Faith should've known that trying to convince her father to let her take her mother to Lagos would be futile. His initial response had been a flat out 'No'. At one point, he had accused her of practically peddling prostitution in Lagos. He'd heard gossip of what unmarried girls who worked in banks did to get new accounts. All her attempts to convince him that she didn't work in a bank fell on deaf ears.

She'd threatened to take her mother anyway without his permission. But it had only been hot air on her part. Her mother would never go against his wishes. She knew that already.

In the end, they'd all agreed on a reasonable compromise, thanks to her mother. They would wait until the results from the hospital came back. And if the doctor gave the all-clear for her to travel, then she would go to Lagos.

Faith agreed to it and left them to spend the night in the hotel she'd already booked a room in. She stayed at the same place each time she visited Benin so the staff were used to her and they always gave her the best available room at the time.

After she checked into her room, she glanced at her phone for message. Apart from a text message from Ebony, she had no other messages. Feeling listless, she called Mark's phone but got his messaging service, instead. Not sure what to say, she didn't leave a message.

She flicked through channels on the small TV and fell asleep on the bed as she read a book. The sound of her phone woke her up. She glanced at the clock as she picked it up. Five past eleven.

"Hello," she answered the phone in a groggy voice.

"Hi, sweetheart, did I wake you?" Mark's voice sounded like a warm baritone.

Her body perked up, even if her brain still worked its way to an alert state.

"I must have drifted off to sleep watching the TV," she said as she sat up in bed.

"Where's everyone else? Your parents? Brother?"

"I left them in the house. I'm in a hotel room."

"Oh. You didn't stay at your parents? Is there a problem? Your mum?" He sounded very concerned.

"No. It's nothing like that. My mum is unwell but we don't know exactly what is wrong. She saw a doctor and they are running tests at the hospital. So we have to wait for the results."

"Is she at a hospital?"

"No. She's at home."

"Sounds like it isn't that serious, then."

"I hope not."

"So, why are you in a hotel room instead of at home with your family?" he asked in a serious note.

Crunch time.

She'd avoided telling Mark about her family for months now, and he'd been patient with her. But even now, she didn't know what to tell him or how much to tell him. His life was so different from hers.

According to Ebony, the Essiens were a close-knit family and they all always stood up for each other. From the times she'd met Mark's parents, she could see they equally loved all their children. Even Felix, who wasn't the birth child of Mark's mother, was treated no differently. He had the perfect family. She didn't.

"Faith, talk to me. What's going on?" Mark's voice had acquired an urgent growl.

"It's a long story." She sighed.

"Sweetheart, you know I've never pushed you to tell me about your family. I've always respected your boundaries. But I know there's something wrong here. You were in a hurry to go to Benin City this morning to see your parents. Now you're there, you tell me you're spending the night in a hotel. I want to know why. I think I deserve to know. I care about you too much not to want to know."

She could sense his tightly reined frustration from his long speech. She couldn't blame him. He'd been very patient with her. He hadn't given up on her. Yet. Something she dreaded. If the situations were reversed, she would've probably given up on him by now. For that, he needed some form of reward. She owed him. Perhaps telling him on the phone would make it easier. She wouldn't have to show her shame in front of him.

"My father kicked me out," she said with a forlorn sigh.

"What?" The shock in his voice made her want to see him right now. "Your father kicked you out of your family house? Why?"

"Actually, that's not strictly true." She heaved out another sigh. "I left home of my own volition. My father just refused to let me back in because I disobeyed him."

"Hang on. Now, I'm totally confused. You got to Benin and had a quarrel with your father?"

She twisted her lips in dry humour. "My quarrel with my father didn't happen today. It started over twelve years ago when I was a teenager living at home. Things got so bad that I had to leave there. But my father didn't like that and he banned me from ever returning to the house. So these days when I come back, I can't stay in there. I have to spend the night in a hotel or return to Lagos the same day."

"You mean your father hasn't forgiven you for something you did years ago?"

"Technically, I haven't asked him for forgiveness."

"Why?"

"Asking him for forgiveness means accepting that what he did was right and I was wrong. I can't accept that. No." She choked back tears.

"I understand," he said. "When I see you again, I'm going to give you one huge hug."

She smiled through her tears. "Thank you."

"I knew you were a very special woman, strong and fiercely independent. But leaving home and taking care of yourself when you were so young? That's pretty amazing. I mean, my brothers and I left home at eighteen to go to University, but we always had our parents' support and love. I can't imagine what it felt for you to be out there on your own."

"Very tough for a while. But I was lucky; I had Ebony's parents. Her mother helped me secure a scholarship to pay my school fees and after the accident when she came back to live in Lagos, I lived with her for a while."

"I didn't know that." He paused. "Now I understand your relationship with Ebony better. You are more like sisters."

"Yes, we are. Although, at one point when we were in school together, I used to envy her because she had everything I'd always wanted—a father who loved her unconditionally and a mother who was an activist. I don't know. I'm a pretty screwed-up person."

"No, you're not," he said. "You're a brave woman who's had to deal with some really tough problems. I wish I could hold you in my arms right now."

He growled in frustration and she smiled.

Suddenly, she didn't want to be alone in a hotel room. She needed Mark. It was always tough on her, going home and seeing her family and yet, not being included and having to watch things from the outside. She wanted to belong, to be included, and made to feel relevant to someone. To Mark. Whenever they got together, he filled the hole in her life, her heart. Albeit temporarily.

"I wish you were here with me, Mark. I miss you."

"I wish I was there, too, sweetheart."

"Do you really have to go to New York tomorrow?"

"I'm afraid so. Hang on." His voice perked up excitedly. "Maybe there's a way around it. What's the name of the hotel you're in?"

She told him, his excitement infecting her and making butterflies flutter in her tummy. "Why do you ask?"

"You'll have to wait to find out." She heard the smirk in his voice, like he knew something she didn't.

"Mark?"

"You'll have to be patient, sweetheart. I'm going to call in a few favours and I'll call you back in about three hours," came his ominous reply before he hung up.

What did he mean? Mark could be so spontaneous. Was he postponing his trip to New York so she could see him when she returned to Lagos? Highly unlikely, considering he'd already mentioned the importance of the trip.

She knew how jumpy investors could be and how much was involved in courting them and convincing them to part with their money for various projects. And Mark proved too savvy to throw away any hard work he'd already put in all for the sake of a few hours with her. At least, she wouldn't jeopardise her business for him. He understood that about her.

So what was he up to? Since she couldn't get back to sleep, she decided to work, instead, and took out her laptop from her bag. She managed to read through reports and produce a strategy summary within the hour. Still unsure of what to do with herself, she dressed and went downstairs to the bar.

"I'm just going to the bar," she said to the man at the reception desk.

"Have fun," he replied as he smiled at her.

The hotel had a nightclub attached to it, so she decided to spend another hour in there while she waited for Mark's call. Perhaps a little dancing would wear her out and she'd be able to sleep later.

She ordered her usual, vodka and coke, but she didn't move from there. She watched the people gyrating on the dance floor. She'd never been much of a dancer although she did dance sometimes. A couple of men tried talking to her and inviting her to the dance floor, but she dismissed them. Luckily, they didn't persist and left her alone.

Another glance at her watch told her she had a further thirty minutes before Mark would call her back. She'd order one last drink before heading back to her hotel room. It would be impossible to try to speak to him on the phone in there, anyway, with the noise from the music.

A man slid up to the bar on her left side. "Let me buy you whatever you're drinking."

She glanced at him and hid her smirk. Fair-skinned and dressed in a snazzy dark suit and red shirt, he reminded of Van Vicker from a Nollywood movie. If she was in the market, he would've been a tad too young for her. She preferred her men to be men, like Mark. She smiled inwardly.

"Thank you for the offer, but I can take care of myself."

"I'm sure you can," he said smoothly. "I've been watching you since you came in. You're beautiful and confident. I like that in a woman."

Definitely a charmer. If she was free and five years younger.

"Thank you," she said as she smiled at him.

"My name is Efe. Do you mind if I know yours?"

She shook her head. "I just came down for a drink."

"It's okay." He smiled, flashing a set of white teeth. "You don't have to tell me. It's just that I noticed you were on your own, and I hadn't seen you here before. I was just trying to be friendly." He tipped his head and turned away.

"I'm sorry. I didn't mean to be rude."

He turned back with a smile. "It's your prerogative."

"My name is Faith." She stuck out her hand.

"It's nice to meet you, Faith."

His hand felt firm and warm but held none of the electricity she experienced with Mark.

He released her hand. "Whoever it is you're waiting for is a lucky man."

She frowned. "I'm not waiting for anybody."

"Shame. Have a good night, Faith," Efe said, before walking away and merging with the dancers on the floor.

The barman placed her drink in front of her and she took out notes from her purse to pay him. But he shook his head. "It's already taken care of."

"By whom?" she asked, surprised. Surely, Efe hadn't already paid for it.

"I did."

The hairs on the back of her neck stood straight and her heart thudded in her chest at the sound of the voice behind her. She swivelled in her chair. Her mouth dropped open, and her purse slipped from her fingers.

"Mark!" The one word slipped from her lips before she went flying across the floor into his arms.

CHAPTER TWELVE

The surprised expression on Faith's face before she launched off the bar stool like a rocket spelled pure classic amazement. Mark wished he could frame it and keep it forever. He stretched his arms out and caught her as she nearly knocked him off balance on his feet, her limbs clinging to his torso.

Tipping his chin over her head, he drew in a deep breath and let out a satisfied sigh. Sunshine and lavender. Boy, he'd missed her. The way her soft curves moulded to his hard frame reminded him exactly how much he'd missed her presence, her scent, her warmth. For a few moments, he just focused on Faith, on the feel of her body against his, on the basic animal instincts she awoke within him. To possess and protect her by equal measures.

The warm caress of her breath fanned his chest through his shirt, her hands like tight bands around his body as if she would never let him go. This was a different Faith from the one always on her guard in Lagos, who didn't like public displays of affection. In Lagos, she wouldn't have clung onto his body with such reckless abandon. She must have really missed him. He wanted to find the nearest dark corner and lose himself in her.

"You came," she whispered against her chest, her voice out of breath and still astonished.

He leaned back and tipped her head up with the pad of his forefinger under her chin. Her eyes shone bright with unshed tears but she wasn't sad. She beamed him a huge smile, lips curled upwards from cheek to cheek.

"I will have to surprise you more often if this is the kind of welcome I get." The warmest welcome he'd ever had from her, considering she always usually held herself until they were in private before letting go. She didn't seem to care at the moment that they were in a nightclub filled with revellers.

He leaned down and pressed his lips to her soft ones, just a brush, intending to end it quickly. But she surprised him and folded her arms around his neck as she opened her lips for him. Succumbing, he couldn't resist the temptation she laid out for him.

Desire flared within his body and he sought her tongue with his, tangling, duelling, rolling with it. They kissed for one long moment until someone bumped him from behind. He groaned and lifted his head.

"We need to get to your room. I don't want an audience for what I'm going to do to you next."

He was panting. Actually panting! God help him. He was in trouble. This woman had his number.

She giggled, picked up her purse from the floor, and took his hand, tugging him towards the exit, her drink forgotten on the bar surface. Mark waved at the barman and followed Faith outside to cross the lobby to the lifts.

Kola sat in one of the chairs in the lobby waiting for him. Due to the last minute nature of his trip to Benin City in the middle of the night, he'd had to pick someone he could rely on completely. And Kola was the most trusted person the family had in their security team. In fact, Kola was a brother. They didn't share any blood ties but the head of security had grown up in the Essien household, raised as one of them.

With a nod, Mark indicated that Kola could retire for the night. Faith looked up at him.

"Don't I know that guy?" she asked after pressing the lift call button.

Mark smiled at her. "Of course you do. That's Kola. I asked him to come with me."

She glanced back at Kola who lifted the glass in his hand in salutation as he nodded back. She smiled at him before tilting her head up.

"How did you get here?" she asked.

Her voice trembled with what he hoped was excitement.

"Don't tell me that the rumours are true?" she continued.

"What rumours?"

"That the Essiens have a private jet."

He barked out a laugh as he tucked her closer to his side. "You should know better than to believe everything you read in the press. If you check through our annual reports, you'll see there are no private jets listed as company assets."

"So how did you get here—" she glanced at her watch, "—it's almost three in the morning."

"I told you I was going to call in a favour. My friend owns a private jet leasing company. He found a pilot willing to fly one of the planes for the right amount of financial incentive, and here I am."

"Gosh. I still can't believe you're actually here. A part of me thinks I fell asleep on my bed and I'm dreaming all this."

He pressed his finger and thumb against the soft flesh on her arm and tugged.

"Ouch. Why did you do that?"

"Sorry, sweetheart." Lifting her arm like a precious egg, he placed a kiss on the spot. "I just wanted to prove to you that you are very much awake and I'm here in the flesh."

She grinned at him as the lift door opened and she stepped in. When the door closed, she pressed against him.

"Talking about flesh." Her hand cupped the fly of his jeans and all the blood in his body seemed to rush down there. "This part seems very pleased to see me."

She squeezed him and he couldn't suppress the deep groan that rose from his belly. A wonder his body hadn't erupted into flames already. Something had happened to the Faith he knew, and he needed to find out what. But he loved this bold and beautiful Faith.

"Once we get into your room, I'm going to show you just how pleased I am to see you."

He cupped her round hips and pulled her into him, wanting her to feel exactly how hot and hard she made him.

"Oh, another round of door sex." She bit her lower lip. "I'm looking forward to that."

He chuckled. "It's been a long day, sweetheart. I'm not sure I'm up to vertical acrobatics tonight. I will settle for a comfortable bed."

She pouted but he couldn't miss the twinkle in her eyes as she feigned disappointment.

"Are you getting too old to keep up with me?" She teased. "Perhaps I should have settled for Efe, instead."

"Efe?"

"Oh, just some guy talking to me at the bar."

"I saw him. He's okay if you're into toy boys, I guess." He teased her in return, banishing the pang of jealousy that roiled in his belly.

He'd watched the guy approach her and watched as she'd dispatched him unceremoniously. He had nothing to worry about when it came to her loyalty. Moreover, her welcome embrace confirmed that she hadn't been interested in the young man.

"Hey, I'm not that old!"

She swung her arm as if to punch him. Luckily, the doors of the lift opened and he ducked out quickly, tugging her along with him.

The card key fell off her hand as she tried to open the door. He took it and let them into her hotel room.

Later, he would remember the first moment she stepped over the threshold and invited him into her hotel room. Despite the location, it felt right. Like he was meant to be there.

All his instincts pealed like clanging bells, his desire flaring, filling him with the unfulfilled need to take her the way it had been the first night in his apartment.

Another look at her and he had to stop himself. She looked so sweet and dreamy. So vulnerable, and he remembered their conversation on the phone and how the need to protect her had sent him rushing out into the night to catch an unscheduled private flight out to Benin City.

He sucked in a deep breath and her scent filled his lungs. She was everywhere—lavender and sunshine—a fragrance that captured him and turned him inside out.

He drew her closer after he shut the door, wanting to get her very essence imprinted into every pore of his body. The feel of her soft and lush curves, he savoured with relish against the hard planes of his body. He buried his nose into the silky strands of her hair, inhaling deeply as he wanted to get her sweetness to soothe his raging passion.

Having her in his arms calmed him somewhat, but not enough. It still took restraint to not lift her into his arms and take her on the spot. She needed sweet loving tonight after what she'd been through.

Lifting his head, he stared into her caramel eyes.

"Your eyes are the most beautiful I've ever seen," he said.

His voice sounded gruff in his own ears. A wonder his tongue still worked appropriately. He would rather use it stroke her skin, especially the seam of her luscious lips.

"Thank you." Her voice thrummed smoky and low, pulling him into an erotic bind.

He could no longer resist. Tilting her head up with the knuckles on his right hand, he lowered his head and traced his tongue along her soft lips, lingering for long moments over her plump bottom lip.

A tremor ran through her body and he felt it at their point of contact on her lips. If he didn't know her well, he'd worry she grew cold from the air conditioner. But he knew her shiver to be pure anticipation pumping in her veins, just like it flowed through his.

A gap appeared between her lush lips, and with such an irresistible invitation, he couldn't hold back any longer. All the words he wanted to say to her, things he wanted to ask her, just vanished, overwhelmed by harsh and all-consuming desire.

He latched his lips onto hers in a kiss both rigorous in strength and tender in performance. Faith gasped and he swallowed up her cry as he slanted his lips and took the kiss deeper, their tongues meshing and tangling. She tasted sweet and decadent all at the same time. And for moments, he lost himself in her taste, not wanting their connection to end.

Fingernails digging tightly into his chest made him realise she clutched at his shirt in an attempt to stay upright, he assumed. Her body trembled in his grasp and he gasped in surprise and held onto her to keep her up, sure that she could feel his hard-as-a-brick arousal against her belly.

"I've got you, sweetheart," he whispered against her cheek as he trailed his lips to her neck.

Her skin was soft, smooth satin, her neck delicate. The warm air from her sigh of pleasure blew against his forehead. She moved restlessly beneath him as he continued his caress of her skin, licking on her collar where the pulse jumped on contact.

He glided his left hand down her back and cupped her bottom, the globe filling his hand with pliant flesh shielded by a layer of silk.

She lifted her leg, corking it over his hip. As if in a synchronised dance, he raised her up and moulded her body against his.

A groan escaped him when her hot, wet mound rubbed against his fly and his trousers suddenly became tighter. The only thing separating his needy flesh from the sweet, soft, incredible pleasure she would give him was the zip of his fly and a scrap of lace between her legs.

In fact, he grew tempted to put his hand between them and release his erection, but remembered he promised himself he would take it nice and slow with her tonight.

Of course, this was no longer night but the early hours of Sunday morning. In a little over an hour, it would be dawn. And he would be on the return flight to Lagos and then onwards to New York later. He wanted to cherish the short time he had with Faith.

He braced them against the door to catch his breath, both hands caressing her bottom slowly as he slipped his tongue into her mouth with the subtlety of a stealth assassin at night.

She rocked against him, sliding her mound over his erection in a desperate motion.

A growl vibrated through him and he ripped his lips from hers.

"If you keep doing that, we'll have a repeat of our first night together," he said as he stared down at her. Her eyes had grown hooded, blazing with lust.

"I told you I liked door sex," she replied and licked her lips in the sexiest manner he'd ever seen.

His arousal hardened and swelled even further, as if he wasn't aching enough.

"Fuck!" He couldn't stop the exclamation, a shout of intent as well as a prayer and a curse.

There suddenly seemed like no air existed in the room, his skin now burning with heat and need despite the air conditioner. His lungs burned and he panted as he wrestled to get back his control. Otherwise, he'd be exploding in his trousers like a teenager.

He did a quick recon of the room, found the bed, and moved in that direction while kissing the corners of her lips. He moved as slowly as he could, tracing every curve with his tongue, and then he nibbled his way down her cheek to her chin.

His leg bumped the edge of the bed and he unceremoniously dumped Faith on it and covered her body with his, not giving her time to catch her breath.

With her back pressed into the top sheet, she turned her head, giving him access to her neck. He groaned as he licked the pulse beating with the force of a marching band in the hollow of her throat.

The salty taste of her sent more heat sizzling on his skin and suddenly, he wanted to be naked, to feel her flesh against his. Sweat broke out on his skin, his heart pounding. Her hands moved to his back, caressing the firm muscles.

He leaned on one elbow and used the other hand to undo the buttons on her blouse. It fell apart revealing lush, flawless caramel skin.

"Did you know I love caramel?" He said the words in his head aloud before dipping down to swipe his tongue on the valley between the globes of her breasts. "Delicious."

He lifted his head. The brown aureoles peeked through the mesh of her lace black bra. He tugged the cups down until they sat beneath the flesh of her breasts, pushing them together as if presenting them to him, her nipples hard points he couldn't resist.

He lowered his head again and sucked in a nipple into his mouth, latching onto a succulent breast, as well. The sound of a groan rent the air and he wasn't sure if it came from him or Faith.

Her fingers clutched his shoulders as her back arched off the bed, pushing her breasts further into his mouth. He repeated the action with the other side and she did the same.

"Mark!" She gasped out his name this time.

Oh, he loved hearing his name on her lips, especially when she moaned it out in pleasure like this. He wanted to hear it again and again. So he continued his attentions. She rocked her body into his and for a moment, he lost control and surged involuntarily into her hips, grinding into her as if they didn't have any clothes between them.

It reminded him he had to get rid of their layers. He wanted to see the rest of her.

Rising to his knees on the bed, he tugged her blouse off her arms and tossed it away from the bed. She reached behind to unhook her bra.

"No. Don't." He shook his head. "I like the way it pushes and moulds your breasts like you're wearing a cupless corset."

She dropped her hands to her sides and lay back as he unzipped the side of her skirt and pulled it down over her hips and off her legs to join the blouse somewhere on the floor.

As he suspected, she wore a scrap of lace masquerading as a thong, with a little triangle covering her sex while showcasing her bare hips and thighs in the most provocative way a piece of fabric could.

He groaned from deep in his chest before running the pad of this right thumb over the lace. His questing digit met hot and slick fabric even before he slipped his finger beneath and met flesh. Scorching and throbbing flesh.

Her whimpers travelled through him like electricity charging him to explore more. He caressed her folds until his finger found her button and she keened.

Hooking his fingers into the edge of the thong, he pulled them off, revealing her sex covered in trimmed hair.

Finally taking off her clothes became his undoing. No way he didn't want to be between her legs now. In a rush of movement, he tugged at his clothes, divesting his body of them as if in a race.

Then he reached for the foil of condom in his wallet and sheathed himself.

Faith rolled her pink tongue over her plump lips and his need rose another notch. The smoky, glazed look of her eyes told him she wanted him as much as he wanted her, as much as the way she parted her legs when he climbed back onto the bed.

He positioned himself, nudging her slick entrance as he lowered his head to take her lips in a kiss that relayed his hunger as well as his affection. Then he thrust in, her tight walls of heat expanding and contracting around him.

She mewled as he groaned, both swallowing each other's cries as he set a slow pace to start, but two strokes in and he was lost. It wouldn't be long now, from the sounds she was making. So he increased the pace, wanting to keep up with her.

Soon, they were both cresting the waves of passion and she clung on to him and cried out his name.

CHAPTER THIRTEEN

"Have you seen this?"

Faith looked up to find Stella strolling into her office, her smart phone in her hand and her expression creased in a frown.

"What?"

"I've just been reading the latest update on the Lori Booth blog," Stella said as she plopped herself onto the chair in front of Faith's desk and leaned forward, her voice lowered conspiratorially.

"You know I don't read that gossip blog. The woman needs to get a life instead of gossiping about what celebrities are up to," Faith replied, not hiding her disdain for the very popular Nigerian gossip blog.

"Well, I know you don't read it, which is why I brought my phone to show you. You wouldn't believe whose picture is on it."

"I really don't care, Stella." She had better things to do and, more importantly, an emergency board meeting to prepare for.

"I think you will care when you see the picture." Stella shoved her phone in Faith's face. "Look at it."

Sighing in resignation, Faith took the phone from her friend and had to refocus her eyes on the small screen.

At first, the image just showed a couple in a half-embrace, with the hand of the man over the woman's shoulder and the woman's arm behind and around his waist. They looked like they were laughing at something or some joke somebody told. At first glance, they looked like a very happy couple as they glanced at each other.

Something about the dimple on the man's face had her looking closer. She picked up her discarded tortoiseshell reading glasses from her desk and put them on before checking the phone again. The image cleared up and she saw their faces.

Her heart stopped and crashed.

No. This can't be right. It's not him.

With haste, she used her forefinger to slide the screen along so she could read the headline for the post.

IS THIS THE NEXT MRS. ESSIEN?

The headline seemed to leap off the screen at her. She dropped the phone on the desk as if it had just bitten her and shook her head.

"Yep, I had that same reaction when I saw that picture and headline," Stella said as she took her phone back.

I bet you didn't, unless you've been sleeping with him, too.

Blood drained from her head and she didn't respond to her friend. Instead, she pulled up the internet browser on her laptop and typed in the blog URL. Somehow, she needed to confirm it wasn't true. She couldn't believe what she'd seen. The image could have been doctored. Photoshop-ed or whatever.

"That Wumi is sneaky. She didn't even tell us they were dating," Stella continued. "And there I was, thinking I might have a chance one day."

As soon as the page came up, the image popped right there on the front page. No mistaking the picture of Mark and Wumi in a bar or nightclub, strobe lights and people around them. They could've been dancing when that picture had been taken.

She scrolled down the page and gasped. According to the details on the column, the picture had been taken a few days previously, the same night she'd been in Benin with Mark.

How could that be possible? Had he crawled out of Wumi's arms and straight into hers? She glanced at her handbag and the packet in it with the stick. Remembered the indicator that signalled she had a new life growing inside her.

This can't be happening. Not now.

"Have you seen Wumi?" She needed some answers.

"No, she wasn't at her desk when I came over. She could be in a meeting."

Faith glanced at her watch. "Shit. I have a meeting to get to, as well." She slammed her laptop shut and picked up her notepad.

"The board meeting. Do you know why there's an emergency board meeting today?" Stella asked as Faith rounded her desk, the picture of Mark and Wumi pushed to the back of her mind.

She needed to be all business now. In a few minutes, she would be sitting in conference with the executive team at City Investments and she needed her bring her winning game, especially since their Managing Director had called this session out of the blue. Unusual but not unheard of, especially when he held an important announcement that would change the future of the firm. She would have to pass on whatever information she garnered to her team.

Confidently, Faith walked to the conference room where the meeting would be held. Kayode Dada, the Information and Technology Director, already sat there and greeted her when she went in. Always smartly attired and good-looking, he was one of the youngest members of the board and had returned from the United States to work for City. She got along well with him and pulled up a chair beside him as they chatted. The Director of Operations and HR, Nathaniel Maduka, an affable man in his forties, joined them next.

David Bode, the finance director, walked in with the managing director, Francis Okolo. They two men were close in age, both in their fifties. Faith tried to read their expressions but neither gave away whether the news would be good or bad.

After they had all exchanged pleasantries and helped themselves with the refreshments laid out for the meeting by personal assistant to the MD, Mr. Okolo began speaking.

"I know you are all wondering why I called this meeting. I won't keep you waiting for much longer." He cleared his throat. "It had always been my intention when I started this firm to take things slow after a certain age. I built this firm from nothing with David. At the time, we both swore to each other that we would work very hard to build up the business and retire early. Well, the time has come."

He paused and a murmur passed between the attendees as they looked at one another. Faith glanced at Kayode and then back at the MD.

"I will be stepping down as MD of City Investment."

"But sir, you're still very young to retire."

"Thank you, Faith." The corners of his eyes crinkled as he beamed a full set of white teeth.

"I will be sixty at my next birthday and there are other things I want to do with my time. Like visiting my children in the US and seeing my grandchildren while they are still babies. There is a time for everything, and I know this is the right time, especially when I know City will be in very good hands."

Faith's heart pounded in her chest. Had he chosen a successor? Was he going to announce the person now? Mr. Okolo's children had little interest in running the business, each with their own successful careers.

"Which brings me to the next point," he continued. "I value each one of you as members of my executive team and the great contribution you make to this firm. You have always been supportive, so I know you will continue giving the same support to the next head of the team.

"The person comes with extensive experience of running a successful financial investment business and I'm excited for the plans for the future." He turned to his personal assistant. "Florence, please show our guest in."

Another murmur went through the room as his PA stepped out. A slight disappointment passed through Faith but she straightened her shoulders as she struggled not to show it. She would've loved to be in the position where she would be considered suitable to head a firm like theirs. In a few years, she would make sure she got considered first. In the meantime, she just hoped whoever he'd chosen would be progressive and open-minded about having a woman in the leaders' team.

"So it is with pleasure that I announce the upcoming merger of City Investment with Apex Financials."

It took Faith a long time for her brain to process the unexpected words from her MD because her gaze had fixated on the man who had just walked into the room. The air in the space shifted, as if displaced by a surge in electricity. A prickly tremor raced down her spine.

"Most of you will already know Mark Essien."

All the men stood and shuffled to introduce themselves or shake his hand, the effect of having an alpha among them.

Faith had to pick her agape jaw off the floor first.

When did he get back from New York? What was he doing here?

Drawing in a long breath to compose herself, she stood and walked to where the men gathered around Mark.

"And this is my protégée and our brilliant strategy and development director, Faith Brown. You will find her an asset on the team," Mr. Okolo said.

"Ms. Brown and I have met and I'm looking forward to working with her."

He held slight amusement in the eyes that stared down at her. Suddenly, the seriousness of what Mr. Okolo had said came crashing down on her.

"You're buying City Investments?" The words came out of her mouth before she could stop them. Groaning inwardly at her loose tongue, she berated herself. Not the right time to let her mouth run away with her.

She stared at Mark, boldly trying to hide her embarrassment as he took her hand. His thumb caressed her knuckles as he released her fingers. She missed his touch as the back of her hand tingled.

"It is more a merger than an acquisition. Mr. Okolo is retaining some shares, although he's not taking an active role in the future business." He stepped back as he addressed the rest of the group.

"I know you all have loads of questions. We will have plenty of time during the due diligence process to deal with queries and concern. For now, I want to reassure you all that I see an exciting future for us all with the merging of our two firms. City has the appropriate expertise in the oil and gas sector and provides a depth of knowledge that will take Apex years to achieve if we were to go into the sector organically. On the other hand, Apex has a reputation within the financial sector that will secure all our futures, no matter the turbulence in untested markets.

"I had promised Francis I would be here when he made the announcement, which is why I've just come over straight from disembarking on a long flight from New York. I've arranged for my PA to contact Florence about setting up one-to-one meeting with each director. I hope to be able to allay any concerns you may have in those sessions. In the meantime, I'll leave Francis to wrap up the meeting."

"Thank you for joining us this morning. I appreciate you coming in, especially after such a long haul flight. I'll see you tomorrow at the Ikoyi Club," the MD told him.

"Hopefully, if I'm not sleeping away the effects of jet lag. It was nice meeting you all," Mark said before stepping out of the door, followed by the MD.

"Did you know this was going to happen?" the operations director asked David.

"He's been thinking about it a lot since his last birthday," the finance director replied. "He always thought he would hand over to someone within City, but when Mark made him a great offer, he couldn't resist."

"This is such shocking news. I wasn't expecting it," Kayode said.

Tell me about it. What is Mark up to? Why was he buying City? The man knew how important this firm was to her and her career. Her shock slowly wore off, turning into anger. Had he used her to find out information about City? Had she let things slip during one of their pillow talks? This was exactly the reason she hadn't wanted to date him in the first place. And if anyone found out she was involved with him, the press would have a field day.

Mr. Okolo returned and the meeting ended. Faith went back to her desk. The more she thought about it, the angrier she got. He hadn't bothered to tell her about his plans, and then there were the pictures of Mark and Wumi making the rounds over the gossip press. And he hadn't even bothered to tell her he was returning to Lagos this morning.

Her phone pinged with a message notification. She swiped the screen.

Meet me for lunch. The car is in the parking lot.

Mark's text message flashed like a red flag before a bull, raising her anger even further. He had some balls. After what he just pulled in the boardroom, did he really think he would click his fingers and she would come running?

Go to hell, she typed out before pausing.

No. What she wanted to say to him, she would do to his face. She backspaced and started tapping the screen again.

I'll be down in 5.

She grabbed her bag and stepped out of her office.

"Amara, I'm taking an extended lunch break. If you need to reach me, I'll be on my mobile."

She didn't stop to see the expression on her PA's face as she headed for the lifts. Downstairs, she spotted Mark's sleek dark Mercedes executive car, glad she didn't have too far to walk under the blazing heat of the midday sun. His black and white uniformed chauffeur stood outside and opened the back passenger door as she approached.

After she stepped into the cool, dark interior, her eyes took a few seconds to adjust to the gloom as the driver shut the door. The shadows gave Mark an air of danger, a lion in his den. A shiver ran down her spine. Male spice scented the air, triggering the instinct to sink into his strong arms. He always had that effect on her.

Enough. She shook off the sensation and stiffened her back.

"Hi, sweetheart."

Opening his arms, he reached for her shoulders. She tilted to the left, dodged his questing fingers, and swung her arm. The slap connected with his bristly jaw.

"Don't call me sweetheart."

"Aww."

One hand clutched his left cheek, the other pressed a button. The tinted partition slid upwards, returning the back interior into shadows with minimal sunlight filtering through the darkened windows. Gentle vibrations beneath the soft, luxurious dark leather seat indicated the car had started moving.

"You lying sonofabitch." Her right palm stung but she swung it a second time.

Firm fingers grasped her wrist mid-air in a vicelike grip.

"Perhaps I deserved the first one, Faith. But you don't get to slap me again unless you want one in return."

Her head ached. She grunted and tugged her arm. His grip didn't loosen.

"Let me go, Mark." Her body vibrated, anger popping in her veins in mini-explosions.

The whoosh of a ragged breath drawn in and out filled the air. He let her hand go. Pushing back in her seat, she sought to put as much distance as possible between them. Averting her gaze, she stared at the traffic light at the junction as it counted down to green. Except at the moment, red mist tinted her vision.

"Faith, what is going on?" His demand had an edge of concern.

She whipped around, facing him. A spotlight highlighted his striking profile. He must have turned it on. Dark eyes bore into hers, scrutinising, yet alluring. The urge to let go and get lost in them—in him—flared, heat flushing her body.

She shook her head, dismissing her body's response to him. "Are you really going to ask me that after the stunt you just pulled in the boardroom?"

Horizontal lines marred his forehead, his eyes narrowed into slits.

"I didn't do anything I haven't been doing since I started running Apex Financials. It was a business decision, and we agreed to keep business separate from our personal relationship."

"Well, you made it personal when you decided to buy City Investments. For goodness' sake, you know how much this job means to me."

"I told you I wanted you to work for me."

His voice gentled, soft as honey, enticing, matching the lazy smile on his face. His warm palm covered her bare lower arm, fingers caressing.

Her skin tingled, nipples beaded, and a slow ache built between her thighs, adding to her already choppy breathing. She lowered her eyelids, took a slow, deep breath, and shook his hand off.

"And I said no. I haven't changed my mind." She met his gaze again.

His eyes marbled, glinting cold and hard. The line of his jaw stiffened, the hard-nosed businessman replacing the charming playboy.

"Then that's a big shame because I'm not going to give up a great opportunity like City."

She flinched, hearing the unspoken words. *"Not even for you."* The pain in her chest announced her shattered heart.

She shut her eyes tight, fighting the tears waiting to spill from behind her eyelids. Why did she ever think their relationship was special? That she could be more than just a notch on his bedpost? *Foolish woman.*

She should've known he would remain ruthless as far as business was concerned. Was that partly why he'd started dating her? Had she inadvertently given him the ammunition to take over her firm?

"How long have you wanted to buy City? Is that why you asked me out, so you could get information from me?"

Her stomach clenched and nausea rose as she asked the question. But she had to know if she'd been a pawn in her own downfall.

"Stop this nonsense." Frustration laced his words.

"Our relationship is the nonsense." Opening her eyes, she glared at him.

"Do not belittle what we have."

"You did that already when you decided that acquiring City was more important than what we have."

"I never said that." His fingers gripping the seat side-rest showed taut knuckles.

"You didn't have to," she replied, her throat dry.

His loud growl reverberated inside the car. It should've been her cue to back off. She didn't.

"How long have you wanted City?"

The space between them disappeared as he loomed over her, her back pressed into the corner of the seat.

"Mark, what are you doing?" Her heart thudded loudly, her breath caught in her throat.

"There's one sure way of shutting you up."

The huskiness in his voice melted her outrage, arousal taking over.

Lean, hard, masculine muscles pressed against her soft flesh, the fabrics separating them inconsequential. The hard points of her nipples chaffed against the lace of her bra. Her body trembled, her hands moistened as her lips parted. But no words came out.

Long fingers curled around the back of her neck, pressing her head forward. "I'm going to kiss you now."

Their lips joined and Faith's fury translated into passion. She kissed him back, her hands clutching his neck. She felt him everywhere as her heart thudded and her breath stalled and she drank as much of him in as possible.

Her left hand slid down and cupped the bulge in his trousers. Mark groaned and pulled back, his eyes blazing as much as hers must blaze, too.

"What are you doing?"

"You are not the only one who can play this game," she bit out in a breathless voice.

"This is not a game." His eyes hardened and he looked pissed off.

"Then answer my question."

He blew out a frustrated breath and shifted back into his seat.

"I'd always admired Francis Okolo and the way he ran City. He is my father's friend. When news of his looming retirement reached me a few weeks ago, I decided to capitalise on it. I made him an offer. He accepted it. No harm done."

She swallowed the lump in her throat and nodded to avoid shedding the tears building up behind her eyelids.

"So while you were fucking me last weekend in Benin, you knew you be taking over City and you didn't think to tell me." She hated how her voice sounded.

"Faith—"

"No." She held up her hand in censure. "No need. I totally get it. Business is business. What we had was just a bit of fun. And now, it's over."

"What?"

"It's over, Mark. It was fun while it lasted. Now, it's time to move on."

"You're not serious."

"I'm as serious as a heart attack. As if everything else isn't bad enough, I have to stomach seeing pictures of you and Wumi splashed all over the internet—"

"Is this about Wumi? You knew I was going to play tennis with her and other friends. Afterwards, we went out for a few drinks. It wasn't just the two of us. There were at least six of us in the group." He scrubbed his head, his frustrations vibrating off his agitated motion. "For goodness' sake, I leased a plane and flew out to you that same night. Do you really think I would flit from one woman to another? On the same night? I am not my father. I have never cheated on you or any other woman!"

The vehemence in his voice bounced off the interior of the car. Faith reared back as if he'd smacked her. She sucked in a deep breath, calming her temper a notch.

"Mark, I believe you. But this is not about Wumi. It's about us. We are not meant to be together. I don't fit in your life, and you don't fit in mine. Full stop. I'm done with this. Take me back to City offices."

His body tensed and when he spoke into the intercom, his voice sounded cold. They sat in a depressing silence for a while, the quiet only interrupted by the occasional jolt from a pothole or the muffled beeping of car horns from outside. Faith braced herself because her bad news for him hadn't ended.

"I have something else to tell you. I want to make it clear that I'm not asking you for anything in return. I'm simply letting you know because I think you deserve to know."

She paused, digging in her handbag for the packet and using the opportunity to gather her wits about her. She held it in her hand for a couple of breaths, puffing in and out. Then, she withdrew the white plastic stick and looked at the text indicator.

Her heart jolted, her insides clenched.

"I'm pregnant," she said and held the stick up.

From the corner of her eye, she saw him flinch before his hand was suddenly on her shoulder, turning her to face him.

"What did you say?"

"I'm pregnant, up the duff, expecting a baby. Here." She thrust the stick into his line of sight.

He stared at it and then at her.

"You're pregnant and you just told me we're over?"

"Yes." She shrugged. "It doesn't change anything."

"Like hell, it doesn't. You're going to have my baby, and you're telling me you don't want me in your life? That's not going to happen."

"Look, Mark. This is not the dark ages. I don't need a man in my life before I can take care of a baby."

"Well, I've got news for you, sweetheart. I'm not just any man, and this is not just any baby." He gave a pointed look at her still-flat stomach. "We are both Essiens. And Essien children don't grow up outside the family."

"Mark, listen—"

"No, you listen. You said your piece. Now, hear mine. I will not rest until you are officially an Essien. We are getting married."

CHAPTER FOURTEEN

Faith couldn't get out of the car fast enough. No point sitting there arguing with a stubborn Mark who remained adamant they had to get married despite her protestations and disagreement.

She'd been sadly surprised at the calm way he'd accepted that they were over. Yet, the moment she mentioned the pregnancy, he'd been quick to claim the child as his and in demanding that their relationship couldn't end now.

She blew out a frustrated breath as she boarded a crowded lift up to her floor. She would show Mark that he couldn't railroad her into anything.

"You're back already." Amara's voice held surprise as Faith entered her office.

"Yes, I completed what I needed to do quickly," she replied distractedly. "Please contact Florence and set up a meeting with Mr. Okolo."

"Did you have any date in mind?"

"If I could see him today, that would be great. Otherwise, first thing tomorrow will be fine."

"Okay."

Amara hooked the phone under her ear as Faith shut her door. She picked up her desk phone and pressed a speed dial button. Each of the directors' direct lines had been keyed into the direct dial buttons. Number three was Kayode's.

The call connected at the second ring.

"KD," she said as soon as she heard his voice. His close friends addressed him by using his initials, and she wanted him to understand that this conversation was purely confidential. "Have you got time for a chat? I have something I need to run by you."

"Sure. I was going to pop over to Lottie's for some lunch. Do you care to join me?"

"Sounds like a plan. I'll see you downstairs in ten minutes."

She hung up and pressed another button on the keypad.

"Hi, Faith. I popped in to see if you wanted to do lunch but Amara said you were out already," Stella said.

"Yes, I had to go out to do something." She fiddled with her wristwatch again. She always felt guilty keeping her affair with Mark secret from her friend. But it seemed that had been a great idea because it was over, anyway. At least, for the time being. Until her pregnancy started showing and everyone began asking her who the father was.

"I need you to run some numbers for me," she said.

"What do you need?"

"I need a P&L forecast for the next 3 years, and a special report on the Energy sectors and sustainability projects in the pipeline."

"When do you need this by?"

"Tonight."

"What? Is Mr. O requesting this?"

"No. It's for a project I'm working on. I'll tell you about it when we discuss your report later."

"Okay." Stella sighed. "I'll get to it, then."

"Thank you. You're a star."

"Yeah, you owe me."

Feeling upbeat despite this morning's news, Faith headed out to lunch with Kayode. She had a plan that would secure City's future and pull the rug out of Mark's takeover bid. He had to learn that two could play his darn game.

Lunch went extremely well. Kayode agreed with her plans as she laid them out. They needed one more member of the leadership team to back their proposal, and then they could move on to the next stage. This would be the difficult part.

While Nathaniel was a good enough Operations director, he and Faith had had enough disagreements in the past for her to know he wouldn't necessarily back her proposal. Naturally, they would have sought the backing of the finance director. But since Mr. Bode was close to Mr Okolo's age and therefore nearing retirement himself, he didn't have a long-term active future in City.

The person next in line as director of finance was Wumi, and if the pictures Faith had seen earlier were anything to go by, she was the last person Faith would invite to back her.

Really a shame, because before Faith had met Mark, she'd had a good relationship with Wumi. Now, she wasn't sure she could class Wumi as her friend anymore.

All because of a man!

"I got you a meeting with Mr. O in the morning." Amara walked into Faith's office as she opened up slides to start working on a presentation.

"Great." The time should be enough for her to prepare her proposal for the MD.

"Will that be all?"

"Yes, thank you."

Amara shut the door as she left and Faith focused on her computer screen.

An hour later, she had the draft ready. She just needed to plug in the financials from Stella and they should be good to go.

Talking about finance, they needed backing, and only one person could help her at such short notice.

She picked up her phone.

"Hello," the voice said on the other end.

"Good afternoon, Mumsie," Faith said.

"Faith, my daughter. *Kedu?*" Mrs. Duru asked.

Faith smiled. "*Odi mma.*" Her Ibo language wasn't great, but this had become a fond greeting ritual of theirs since Faith went to live with Ebony's mum as a teenager.

"Good. How are your parents and your brother, Odion?"

"I saw them two weekends ago. They are well. Well, my mum had to see a doctor because she hadn't been feeling well. But she seems all right at the moment."

"Oh, I hope it was nothing serious. If there's anything I can do, just let me know."

"Thank you, Mum." She paused as she composed her thoughts. "There is something I need your help with."

"Tell me. I'm all ears."

Faith told her about what had happened in the boardroom this morning and her ideas for the future of City. She left out details of her involvement with Mark, not ready to explain it to anybody, yet.

"That's quite an ambitious plan you have there," Mrs. Duru said. "But if anyone can pull it off, I know you will. So I'm going to help you and connect you with some financiers who can back you."

"Oh, thank you, Mumsie." A huge breath she'd been holding whooshed out of her mouth as she nearly hopped off her chair with joy and excitement.

"I'll call you back later with the names of the contacts."

"Okay, Mum. Thanks again."

Mrs. Duru hung up. Faith was pumping her hand through the air when Stella walked in.

"You look happy," her colleague said as she sat down. "What's got you so excited?"

"Some great news to brighten a day that started dismally," Faith said, not hiding the huge grin on her face. Perhaps she could actually pull this whole thing off and provide a great future for her and her unborn child without Mark.

"Come on, spill. First, you make me do this report in record-breaking time." She dropped the folder she held on the desk. "Now, you look like you've just won the lottery."

"Close, my sister. Close." Faith pulled her chair out so she could sit side by side with Stella. "You're a close friend of mine and I would really love to get you on board, so I'm telling you this under strict confidence. You can't tell anyone about it, at least, not until after tomorrow, do you understand?"

"Sure. I understand. I won't tell anyone."

"Good." She paused for a breath. "I'm organising a management buyout of City."

Stella stared at her with a frown on her face for a few seconds. Faith could see the moment the penny dropped.

"Oh my God. You're not. Really?"

"Yep. That's why I needed the reports. KD has agreed to it, and I just got off the phone with someone organising financiers."

"Wow. Girl, I have a new respect for you. I don't know if I could do it. Go up against a man like Mark Essien? No way. He's one ferocious beast."

"Yes, but even lions have tamers."

"Touché."

"So, what exactly do you need me for?"

"We need a financial whizz, and you're it."

"Aren't you better off with Wumi? She's deputy Finance Director and she'll probably be taking over as Finance Director once Mr. Bode steps down."

"Yes, but as your pictures from this morning proves, she's already consorting with the enemy." *And I don't trust her.*

"Good point. But you know I'm just an analyst."

"Stop putting yourself down. You're the best senior analyst at City, and probably one of the best in the whole of Nigeria. One day, you'll head the department and that day is fast approaching, in my opinion."

If it was possible for her dark skin to turn red, Faith was sure Stella's would be crimson now by the smile she was giving her. The girl always belittled her own qualities.

"Thank you, Faith."

"You're welcome. So are you in?"

"Of course, I'm in."

"Great. Let's get to the report, then."

Stella walked her through the report she'd prepared. By the time Mrs. Duru called her back, she had a strong grasp of the future potential of City. She got the phone number of one of the people who could possibly finance her venture.

That night, sleep didn't come easily. Without the stress of preparing the proposal and worrying about raising finance, she remained with her thoughts of Mark. Each time she closed her eyes, an image of him loomed large.

The memory of turning around and seeing him in that nightclub in Benin, and of the sweet, slow way he'd made love to her that night left her hot and needy. How could he be so thoughtful and gentle with her one minute and yet so ruthless another?

Was it really so easy for him to keep a clear demarcation between his business priorities and personal relationships? Perhaps she hadn't meant that much to him, after all. Perhaps he hopped on a flight to any girl in the middle of the night.

She pounded her frustration into her pillows, vowing not to cry over the loss of their relationship. She would get over him. She had to focus on securing City. Once that was done, she would concentrate on preparing for the birth of her baby. If everything worked out, she would be able to pay for a nanny to take care of the child so she could get back to work quickly after her maternity break.

This thought finally put her to sleep. In the morning, she was dressed and in the office even earlier than usual.

At her scheduled time, she was in Mr. Okolo's big, spacious air-conditioned office filled with dark wood and old books.

"Faith, come in," he said when she greeted him. He ushered her towards the set of sofas on the other end of the office. "Would you like a drink?"

"Water would be fine," she replied.

Florence left to bring the drinks as Faith settled in the soft, tan leather sofa and crossed her legs at the ankles, pushing them to one side as she sat on the edge of her seat. She couldn't afford to relax until she'd achieved her aim.

Mr. O sat opposite her and spread himself. Florence returned with a bottle of cold water on an aluminium tray with two tall, clear glasses. She filled them and left.

"I know yesterday's news came as a surprise to you. When Florence said you wanted to see me, I asked her to book you in for the earliest spot. How are you coping with it?"

Silently, she thanked God for his intuition. It would make things a little easier for her.

"Thank you, sir. I'm doing okay, although I'm worried."

"What exactly worries you, my dear?"

"Well, sir, I'm worried this merger will mean job losses for a lot of staff and changes to the ethos at City."

"We haven't worked out the details yet as this is still early stages, but Mark assures me that any job losses will be a minimum."

"Sir, think about the loyal people who have worked for this firm for years and have contributed in making it what it is. How do you think any one of them will feel to lose their job? I know that I wouldn't like to be the one tossed out."

"Oh, you don't have to worry about that, my girl. Mark will be a fool to let someone as brilliant as you out of his grasp."

Faith blushed under the double-edged meaning of his words although she didn't think he realised its effect on her or that she and Mark had a relationship outside of business. Was that Mark's plan through buying City? Trying to keep her within his grasp?

Mentally, she shook her head and continued. "Over at Apex, they don't have any women on their executive team. Have you considered that maybe I might be the first person to go with this new merger?"

"Hmmm." Mr. Okolo scratched his clean-shaven chin. "I hadn't thought about that. Look, I'll get him to sign an undertaking that states he should keep you on the leadership team as part of the merger."

"He might resent me for that. No, thanks, sir. I have a better idea." She paused, waiting for his response.

"You do? Let's hear it." He waved her on.

She flipped open the file she had in her hand and handed it over to him as she brought up the proposal on her laptop.

"I've been looking at the numbers and our future plans and I think I can come up with the finance to buy you out. That will leave your business intact and still allow you to retire early."

He reared back, stared at her then at the folder in his hands, and then back at her, before beaming a wide smile.

"I'm listening."

Breathing a sigh of relief, she ran through the presentation, highlighting the key points and benefits for him and the company.

"You did all this—" he stared at his gold wristwatch, "—in less than twenty four hours? I'm truly impressed."

"Thank you, sir."

"So, tell me, how are you going to get the finance to back up your plans?"

"I have meetings set up with financiers, and I'm hoping to secure the finance in a few weeks. I just need you to hold off from signing anything with Apex until then."

"That is a long time to keep my plans on hold for something that might not materialise. Mark made me a very good offer. It'll be silly of me to turn him down."

"Sir, please just give me some time to get this done."

"Faith, I like you a lot. When I interviewed you for a job with my firm, I saw your potential as being a future Managing Director. I'm just not sure you are ready for it yet. On the other hand, if you can secure finance to buy me out by Friday, then I will reconsider."

"Friday? That's three days away."

He nodded. "Exactly. If you want the role of an MD, you'll need to learn the responsibilities of an MD. If you can secure the finance in time, you can have the job."

He was giving her a chance. Crazy and risky, but she would take it.

"Thank you, sir. I really appreciate you giving me this opportunity."

She refrained from hugging him despite the impulse. Outside, a huge smile played on her lips all the way back to her office and for the rest of the day. She met with Kayode and Stella to update them. They both shared her optimism. For the first time since the board meeting the previous day, she felt like she could actually pull this off.

Her phone rang as she was preparing to go out to meet one of the financiers that Mrs. Duru had set up for her. The caller ID said Mark. She debated whether to answer it as the call continued on. Eventually, she picked it.

"Mark." Even saying his name proved difficult for her and she swallowed a lump in her throat to stop her voice from catching.

"How are you doing? Are you okay?"

His voice came out soft, husky, and nearly her undoing. Not good. This caring Mark could break down her walls so easily.

"I'm well." She took another gulp of air and let it out slowly. "Pregnancy is not an illness, you know."

She heard his soft sigh.

"I know. But I've been reading up and it says some women experience sickness in the early months."

That shocked her. Of all the things she'd been expecting to hear from him, it wasn't this. A part of her hardened heart melted.

"You've been reading up on pregnancy?"

"Yes. I wanted to know what to expect so I can be ready."

"But, I told you not to worry. I'm perfectly capable of taking care of myself and the baby."

"I know you are capable." He heaved a frustrated sigh. "I don't want to argue with you, Faith. Have dinner with me tonight."

"I don't think that's a good idea."

"We need to talk. Just the two of us, without angry words. Please. We can go out if you don't want to come to mine."

His voice thrummed with emotion and she couldn't help caving in.

"Okay. But I can't do this week. There's a lot on my plate. Maybe we can meet up for lunch on Saturday."

A pause came on the line. For a moment, she thought he'd hung up. "Mark?"

"If that's the earliest you can see me, then I'll take it. I'll send you a text message when I've made the arrangements. See you on Saturday."

"No problem. See you then."

The abrupt way the call ended became a sad reminder of how quickly things had deteriorated between them in the space of twenty-four hours. Even though her heart ached for his love and her body for his lovemaking, she couldn't relent now when she hovered so close to her goal.

By Saturday, she would be the one with the upper hand when it came to the future of their relationship.

CHAPTER FIFTEEN

By Wednesday night, Mark couldn't stand being in the same town as Faith and not seeing her. He was having a hard time respecting her wishes and giving her space when all he wanted to do was to touch her.

"I just want to see her," he said to his brother sitting next to him in the private lounge of their favourite haunt. He couldn't shake the depressing fear and resentment he'd felt as a child when he'd lived in the same city and couldn't see his father for weeks on end. Now, those same feelings blanketed him, slumping his shoulders.

"See her?" Felix said, his tone loaded with amusement and innuendo.

"Yes." He couldn't hide his frustration. "Is that too much to ask?"

It wasn't even about sex, although that would be great. He just wanted to hold the woman who carried his unborn child. They'd made a baby. He was going to be a father. Still coming to terms with the fact, he'd been floored by the news.

But to be told in one breath he was going to be a father, and then in another breath, denied permanent access to said baby, rankled. Fear. Frustration. Rage. He'd run the gamut of emotions.

He scrubbed his face and puffed out a deep breath. "Do you remember those days when we were still little and lived apart?"

Felix's face puckered in a frown, his eyes going cold. Mark could imagine the memories flitting through his brother's mind. Dark, painful memories of betrayal and disappointments.

"I hated not seeing Dad often enough." His jaw tightened as he remembered, his temples throbbing with pain. "I resented and blamed you for stealing my father. That was before you saved me from bully Bami Jones and knocked him out in the playground."

Mark lowered his head into his hands. His brother's hand settled on his shoulder. Not a squeeze. Just his presence. Like he'd always been for as long as he could remember. Sedate and reassuring.

"You know it's not your fault," Felix said. "We were both young and we both needed our father, albeit in different ways. We were both disappointed and betrayed by the adults in our lives."

"I realised that much later. But I've always wondered how you could easily forgive me or Dad or my Mum? I mean, you lost the most and yet, you were able to forgive the most."

"It's from my mother. She taught me that forgiveness doesn't mean acceptance of the offence. But when you forgive an offender, it frees to live the rest of your life fully. It's like a reset button in your mind."

"That is so true. You know I've carried this resentment for years. But since I met Faith, it's like I'm finally letting go. I'm finally free. Now she wants to do the same thing to me. If she goes through with her plans of bringing up our child on her own, that will be another child going through the pain and disappointment of not having his or her father."

His brother tilted his head and scratched the bristles on his chin as scrutinised him further.

"You're in love with her." Felix's statement came loaded with surprise.

He let out a ragged breath. "Yes."

The realisation had come to him as he sat in his lonely hotel room overlooking Central Park missing Faith. The shock of it had sent him downstairs to the hotel bar seeking female company to disprove what he hadn't wanted to accept. But nobody else had held a candle against her.

"It took me a while to wrap my head around it, but I do. And she wants to break up with me, all because I made an offer for City Investments."

"You should've told her about it. Instead of springing it on her with everyone else."

"I would've, but she was the one who insisted we should never discuss business when we're in private. She made the rule, damn it." And now, he was the one paying the price for keeping to her rules.

"That's women for you." His brother took as sip of his brandy. "If it's any consolation, I'm still learning new things about Ebony everyday and we're married."

"Well, that's the thing. I would like to marry Faith. But she said point blank no. Can you imagine that? She's carrying my child, for goodness' sake."

Every time he remembered their conversation in the back of the car, his blood boiled. How could one woman be so adamant?

"I feel your pain. But according to Ebony, that was hardly the most romantic proposal of the century."

Mark let out a groan. "Between her slapping me, then telling me we were over before delivering the unexpected news of her pregnancy, I was hardly in the frame of mind to be romantic. I was simply grasping at straws, trying to hold on to the illusion of her."

He shivered as the desperation he'd felt in that moment resurfaced. He'd flown back from New York with the intention of confessing his love for Faith, only to have her practically tell him to piss off. His response had been wrought with anger and despair at losing her *and* their child.

He lowered his head, clutching it in his hands.

"She slapped you?"

Mark raised his head to find amusement in his brother's eyes and his body shaking like he was trying to hold back his laughter. He wasn't succeeding because Mark started laughing out loud as he nodded.

"Yes, she did."

Felix didn't hold back his laughter and they both let it rip. Quite cathartic just letting go after the frustration of the past few days with Faith. He'd known hanging out with his older brother would help him to see things in perspective.

"She is one hell of a babe. You've met your match, brother."

"Don't I just know it. And that's not even the worse of it."

"Dare I even ask?"

"You won't believe it. She's putting in a counter bid for City."

"She did what?"

"I couldn't believe it when a close source told me she'd been talking to financiers about raising funds to buy Mr. Okolo's stake in the business. I called him up and he confirmed that he'd received a counter offer, although he didn't say from whom."

"You've got to marry her. A woman with the guts to stand up to you needs to be on our side, not playing against us. She'll fit right in with us Essiens."

"I absolutely agree. I just need to figure out how to get her to see that I'm not the enemy."

"Seduction, my brother. Lay on the Essien charm."

"I will have to get her in the same room for that to work. But at the moment, she's avoiding me." He paused and scratched the stubble on his chin. "Of course, all it would take would be one phone call and the doors to her financiers will shut down and she will have to come back to talk to me. If she wants to play with the big boys, she should be prepared to get rough and dirty."

"This is where I issue a disclaimer," Felix said in mock seriousness. "I value my marriage and Ebony will keep me in the spare room for a month if she found out I knew you were going to do that and I didn't do anything to stop you. So this is me attempting to stop you. That tactic will work by putting City back in your hands but you might end up losing Faith for good. Don't say I didn't warn you."

"What else am I supposed to do? The woman has me over a barrel—" Something caught his eye by the entrance of the bar. "Speaking of the little feminine devil."

Faith stood by the entrance to the restaurant in a dark green, shift linen dress and diamante strappy stilettos with a matching clutch purse. She looked around as if she expected to see someone. Recognition dawned on her expression as she gave a little wave and sashayed over to a table.

A bronze-skinned man stood in a flamboyantly embroidered navy suit. Mark's blood ran cold as he recognised the guy.

"Isn't that Faith with Kris Petersen?" his brother asked.

"Yes. I can't believe she's talking to that slime ball."

Petersen had a reputation for being a shark and for his unscrupulous business practices. He also had a reputation for his wild sex parties and the man must be in his fifties, for goodness' sake. Not to mention that he had been involved in blackmailing Ebony and trying to oust Felix from his position as Head of Apex Private Bank.

Now, seeing him sitting so close to Faith made Mark want to toss him out of the venue.

Mark tossed back his drink, instead.

"I'm not going to sit here and watch them all night," he said as he stood.

"Don't do anything stupid. We can go."

Mark glared at his brother. "I don't care about doing anything stupid. I just don't want him anywhere near Faith."

He headed for the stairs leading downstairs and to Faith. Behind him, he could hear Felix settling their bill.

Downstairs, Petersen saw him first as Faith had her back to him.

"Mark Essien. Fancy seeing you here."

The fool of a man tried to play coy with him. Petersen knew very well this happened to be his favourite place to hang out. His brother, Tony, owned the bar and restaurant.

Faith's body stiffened as she turned her head to look at him.

He placed his hand on the exposed skin of her back where her neck connected with her shoulders. A proprietary gesture. He no longer cared about keeping his relationship with her a secret.

"Petersen, I need to speak with Faith."

"Mark, we can talk later," Faith said. "We're in the middle of something here."

He looked down to find her glaring at him. "No. We can't talk later. It's urgent." He applied pressure to his hand on her back.

"Kris, please excuse me. I won't be long." Faith stood.

"No problem." Petersen flashed his teeth like a shark. "I'll order some wine for you."

Mark kept his hand on her back as he directed her into the hallway leading to the back office. When she stiffened, refusing to move further, he backed her to the wall, his hands on either side of her face.

"What are you doing with Petersen?"

"It's none of your business, Mark."

"Really?" He eyed her. "Does he know you're carrying my baby?"

This close, her scent surrounded him, drawing him into her. His trousers tightened and his pulse thundered in his ears.

She shifted on her legs and lowered her gaze, swiping her lower lip with her pink tongue. The temptation proved too good to resist.

Leaning forward, he drew that same lip between his. She gasped, giving him an opening which he took advantage of. The last time he'd tasted her had been in the limousine a few days ago, but it felt like a lifetime.

With his hand on her nape, holding her still, he ravished her mouth. She matched his thrust with hers. For each cut, she parried; for each advance, she countered. Her hand moved up his chest. Even through the fabric, she branded him.

It drove him wild. Faith had never been submissive and he loved her for it. But they were best when they worked in sync, not against each other.

He placed his head against hers, both of them panting to catch their breaths.

"Stop fighting me, Faith," he said in a growly voice.

"So you can chain me to your kitchen sink?" Her voice came out choked with emotion.

He lifted his head and studied her face. Her eyes were feverish and over-bright. She seemed to have the same desperate energy that coursed through his veins.

"Right now, all I want to do is chain you to my bed."

Desire flared in her eyes. "Sex doesn't solve every problem."

"It's a good place to start."

He stroked his knuckles against the skin on her neck where it met her shoulder. Her pulse jumped and she closed her eyes. Great to know she still responded to his touch instantly.

"And I've missed you."

"Mark."

The sound of his name on her lips became his undoing. He needed to let her go or he'd be taking her right here.

"It's okay. I'll let you get back to your dinner date. But beware of making a deal with the devil, Faith. I'll see you in a couple of days."

He turned and walked out, refusing to look back, knowing he might not be able to let her go otherwise. Felix waited for him at the exit.

"Are you okay?" Felix asked him as they got into the car.

"I will be once this whole affair is over and she's my wife."

Faith had to suck in a few gulps of air before she could catch her breath after Mark left her in the hallway. It didn't help that the air in the space was filled with his scent—spice and masculinity. That she hadn't caved in and begged him to nail her to the wall as he took her hard must be a minor miracle.

Gosh, she missed him. Seeing him again had reminded her how much.

Straightening up, she headed back into the restaurant. Mr. Petersen had chosen a secluded corner table that gave them some privacy in an otherwise busy top nosh eatery. In fact, she'd been surprised when he'd chosen this place as the venue for their meeting. She knew the place as a favourite haunt for the Essiens; after all, Tony Essien owned it.

So the probability of running into Mark had been high from the start. But she'd assumed Mr. Petersen didn't know the Essiens that well. Although, that would be highly unlikely. Any investor worth their salt knew about the Essiens or, at least, their business influence.

"Sorry about that," she said as she settled back into her chair opposite Petersen.

"Don't worry about it." The man waved off her apology. "Would you like some wine?"

"If you don't mind, I'd like to stick to just water for now. I need a clear head." She didn't want to reveal her pregnancy to anyone yet. Not until her future stood on more solid ground.

"Of course," he replied and poured some of the South African Rose wine into his glass.

A smile curled her lips. Mark had introduced her to South African wines. It seemed Mr. Petersen also enjoyed wine from the region, too.

"What is funny?" he asked as he returned the bottle to the ice bucket.

"I'm a recent convert to South African wine, so it's a pleasant surprise that you chose one."

"I was born in South Africa, on the Western Cape. Worcester, to be exact, although I've spent the last thirty years living in Nigeria."

"Wow. Don't you miss it?"

He shrugged. "Not really. I do travel there quite often. But these days, Nigeria is my home. When I came here in my twenties, I fell in love with the place. Moreover, I have family here now, so the more reason to stay."

She glanced at her notes on her tablet. The information she had on Petersen indicated he wasn't married. Perhaps he meant a live-in spouse.

"I didn't realise you were married," she said, hoping she would find out more about the man she would have as a business partner.

"I'm not. I came close to getting married once." His grey-hazel eyes glazed over. "But that was a very long time ago."

"I'm sorry." She'd heard hurt in his voice.

"Don't be. I was young and foolish and broke. She chose to marry a wealthy man, instead. She did me a favour, really. I swore that I would become very rich and these days, I am. I can buy anything I want."

Despite the bravado in his speech, she still felt something missing. As if he tried to say he could buy anything and perhaps one day buy back the woman he once loved.

But she dismissed the thought. Pregnancy was screwing up with her head and making her read meaning into things that weren't there. Right now, all she was interested in would be securing the money she needed for her counterbid for City Investments.

Of all the other investors she'd chatted with, only Petersen had decided to get to the next stage once they'd found out they would be going against Mark Essien. None of them had wanted to make an enemy of Mark. It seemed Petersen was the only man not afraid of the Essiens.

"Which brings me to buying City," the man said. "I read your proposal and I think you have a very good plan. I am willing to back you with the funds you need."

"Wow, thank you so much." A huge smile split her lips as relief washed over her body.

"Don't thank me yet. I have a couple of stipulations."

"Okay." She held her breath.

"I'm going to get my lawyer to draft a contract ready for Friday."

"That's not a problem. I'm looking to get this deal done immediately. I need the funds ready by Friday, anyway."

"Good. The second thing is that I want shares with a buy-back option only available after two years."

"Sir, my proposal had the buy-back time option as six months."

"Well, Faith...it's okay if I call you by your first name?"

"Yes, sure."

"Faith, you know, I'm investing a lot of money, and you are a relative unknown in the business, so I'm putting a lot of 'faith' in you" He air quoted the word faith. "I want to be sure that my investment yields a good return before you can buy me out, so I think two years is very reasonable."

"How about a one-year option as a compromise?" she asked, not willing to give away so much outside of her original proposal.

He fingered his goatee as he scrutinised her. "I like your spirit, Faith, so here's what I'm offering. Eighteen months, with an increase in shares of ten-percent."

"First of all, sir, that proposal is so good that the Essiens want to get a hold of it. I'm going to make you a lot of money in a short time. So I'm willing to settle for twelve months buy-back and a five-percent increase in shares."

"You drive a hard bargain. But I will take it." He extended his hand.

"Thank you, Mr. Petersen. You won't regret it." She shook his hand firmly. Something niggled at the back of her mind at how easily he caved in to her offer. Had she negotiated too low? Could she have gotten more out of him?

"I hope not." He took out his phone. "Excuse me while I call my lawyer to get work on the contract started."

She nodded and excused herself. In the ladies', she called Stella and told her the news. She was going to meet the deadline Mr. Okolo had set her, after all.

The rest of dinner with Mr. Petersen went smoothly.

The next morning, a copy of the contract landed in her inbox. She sent a copy to her lawyer and read through it. She found nothing in it that she hadn't already discussed and agreed to with Mr. Petersen. After meeting with the rest of the people who would form part of the new leadership team at City, they agreed the contract looked good.

That evening, she signed the contract in Petersen's office in the presence of both lawyers. She declined the celebratory glass of champagne and settled for a glass of sparkling water instead and headed home so she could have a clear head for her meeting with Mr. Okolo the next day.

At ten am on Friday morning, Faith walked into Mr. Okolo's office with confident steps.

"Faith, come in. How are you doing?" he asked her from the other side of his desk as he stood.

"I'm doing very well, sir." She smiled.

"Good," he said and settled into the sofa before waving for her to take a seat.

She sat down opposite him and folded her legs to the side, crossing them at the ankles.

"At the start of the week, I set you a challenge. How is it going?" he asked as he leaned back into the brocade-upholstered sofa.

"Very well, sir. I have the funds for the management buyout."

"You have?" His bushy brows arched high.

She smiled, pleased she had surprised him, and reached into the folder she had placed on the table. "Here is a letter from my bank with proof of the funds available for the transaction."

She handed him the sheet of paper with the bank's embossed logo and stamp. His eyes widened into saucers.

"Amazing!" He looked from the paper to her and back to the paper. "You have surprised me. I knew that if I challenged you, you would rise to the challenge." He handed her back the sheet.

"But I wasn't expecting it to be done. In fact, I thought you'd come asking for an extension of the deadline and I was going to give it to you, anyway, because I knew the timescales were tight." He shook his head and smiled at the same time.

"Really?"

"Yes. But you have exceeded my expectations. Since you have the funds, you certainly deserve to be the next Managing Director of City Investments."

"Thank you, sir."

"But I have to ask, where did you get the money?"

"Does it matter, as long as you get your money and can retire?"

"Perhaps not. But I would hope that you didn't get involved in anything unscrupulous to get the money. Ambition is great. But integrity is better."

For the first time since she signed the contract with Petersen, Faith's joy became tainted with doubt. Mark had warned her about getting involved with Petersen, and now, Mr. Okolo implied she'd acquired the money through foul means.

Her blood boiled. What was it with men, anyway? Her father had been the same. He thought she prostituted her body in Lagos and that was how she made her money.

"Sir, I don't like the implications of what you're saying. You know I would never stoop so low."

Mr. Okolo sighed and leaned over to pat her hand. "I do not mean to upset you. You know I think of you as a daughter, and I would never wish anything bad on you. I'm just worried that getting the funds so quickly would cost you a price too dear."

"I understand, sir."

"Good. I will call a meeting of the senior team this afternoon and we can announce it to them. Of course, it will take longer to work out the details but, congratulations, Faith. I am pleased for you."

"Thank you, sir."

Elated, she walked out of his office practically floating. On her way back, she grabbed Stella and barely concealed her news until she closed the door to her office.

"We got it," she said.

"Oh my God!" Stella shouted and they hugged each other, jumping up and down.

"I can't believe this is actually happening."

"I'm so pleased for you," Stella said, grinning from ear to ear. "You are going to be my new boss."

"And you're going to be the next Finance Director—"

Faith's office door burst open and she swivelled to find Wumi standing there.

"You bitch!" Wumi said as she stormed in and slammed the door shut.

"What?" Faith gasped.

"You've been fucking him." Wumi stood in her personal space, her hands balled by her side and her face contorted in anger.

"What's going on, Wumi?" Stella asked, looking from one woman to the other.

"*You* ask the woman who has been sleeping with my boyfriend."

"I don't know what you're talking about, Wumi." Faith tried to keep her tone neutral but her voice came out with a squeak.

"You don't know what I'm talking about, *abi*?" Wumi snapped her fingers in the air. "Okay. Wait. I will show you." She pulled out a phone from her pocket and fiddled with the screen before shoving it in Faith's face.

Faith squinted and pulled her glasses from her desk to see properly.

MARK ESSIEN SEEN WITH MYSTERY WOMAN IN BENIN CITY.

Her heart thudded in her chest as she looked at the image on the screen. The face of the woman hugging Mark Essien at a bar looked slightly obscured, but Faith recognised herself immediately and heat flooded her face.

She scrolled down to read the rest of the post on the Lori Booth blog.

Bad boy playboy Mark Essien seen at a nightclub in Benin City with a mysterious woman while it is rumoured that he is engaged to childhood friend, Wumi Adekunle. He was featured last week enjoying the company of said fiancée at the Reams nightclub. But it seems Mr. Essien cannot shed his bad boy ways even with marriage looming.

Can anyone name and shame this mystery woman?

Nausea churned her stomach and her head swam. Faith wanted the ground to open up and swallow her. Now, she was being labelled 'the other woman' because people didn't know that Mark and she were an item and Wumi was the one encroaching on another woman's territory.

Her blood boiled with rage and she spluttered, "He is not your fiancé!" before she could think better of it and shoved the phone back at Wumi.

But the open-mouthed shock on both Wumi and Stella's faces made her regret her words.

"So you are not denying it, you shameless woman."

"There's nothing to deny." She turned her back and walked to her desk, wanting some distance between her and Wumi before she would do something she would later regret.

"Look at that." Wumi handed the phone to Stella. "And tell me if I'm not right."

Stella frowned as she stared at the phone. When she looked back up, Faith thought she glimpsed sadness in her eyes.

"Is it true? Are you sleeping with Mark Essien?"

Faith couldn't lie to her friend so she answered, "Yes."

Stella's face fell in disappointment and Faith's heart clenched.

"But it's not what the blog post is making it out to be. Mark is not engaged to Wumi. Never has been. Never will be."

"That's a lie. How come I was in his family home for dinner the other week and we've been hanging out together playing tennis and stuff?"

"I know his mother invited you to dinner without Mark's permission, and I know you used to play tennis before. But I'm the one he asked to marry him and I'm the one expecting his baby!"

The two women in front of her gasped. Wumi covered her mouth, opened the door, and ran out. Faith wished she hadn't blurted out about the pregnancy. But now with the cat out of the bag, she could not go back. She just hoped she hadn't lost her friendship with Stella, as well.

Slowly, she walked over to the door and shut it. When she turned around, Stella was standing behind her.

"I have to go," Stella said, avoiding eye contact.

"Please don't go," Faith said. "I'm sorry."

"Why didn't you tell me? All this while, you've been going out with him, and you never said a word."

"I was avoiding bust ups like this. I didn't want it to be all over the news that I was dating Mark Essien and people speculating if I was going to be the next Mrs. Essien."

"But you are going to be. You are pregnant and he asked you to marry him."

Faith sighed. "He did, but I turned him down."

"Woman, you have to be crazy. You turned down a proposal from a king of Finance? Why?"

At this moment, thinking about the reason she'd said no seemed so trivial.

"I was angry at him for wanting to buy City Investments without telling me first. I guess I was just lashing out."

"I can see how that would piss you off. But do you love him?"

"Sadly, I do."

"And does he love you?"

"I don't know. I don't think he cares about me after that stunt he pulled."

"It seems to me a man like Mark won't propose to a woman unless he really cares about her. You might want to reconsider. Unless you really want him to marry Wumi."

The clenching around her heart tightened. For sure, she wanted Wumi nowhere near Mark. This left her confused. What did she want from Mark?

She sighed and slumped into her chair. Her mobile phone started ringing.

"I'm going to leave you to it," Stella said and headed for the door.

"Thank you for understanding."

"That's what friends are for." Stella smiled and shut the door behind her.

She recognized her brother's caller ID before she picked up the phone.

"Odion, is everything all right?" she said as soon as she pressed the answer button.

"Sister, it's Mum. She's really sick."

Those words sent Faith's world careening out of control.

CHAPTER SIXTEEN

The weekend didn't come fast enough for Mark. For starters, things didn't get any smoother. Friday brought more pictures of him in the gossip press to add to the one already circulating with him and Wumi. This time, it was of him and Faith in the nightclub in Benin while she had been hugging him.

Faith's face looked slightly obscured in the photo but anyone who knew her well would recognise her from the angle.

In a way, he was glad whoever had taken the photo had handed it in to the press. At least, it quashed the rumours of an involvement between him and Wumi. He had never been interested in the woman.

He'd booked them a table for lunch in the private lounge at Reams. It would give her the peace of mind that they couldn't get too intimate but still provide him the privacy he needed to talk to her without interruptions.

"Everything is set for your date," Tony said when he arrived at the restaurant. The place already teemed with lunchtime patrons.

"Good," he replied as his brother led him up to the private corner. The table had been set for two, covered in a cream brocade tablecloth, bone china plates, and silver cutlery. The glasses were crystal. The drapes had been drawn to provide an intimate setting with tens of candles lit all around the space.

If this wasn't romantic, he didn't know what would be.

"I've asked the waiter to bring her straight up here the minute she arrives."

"Thank you, Tony."

Mark didn't sit down. He paced from one end of the lounge to the other. Tony sat astride a chair, his hands leaning against the back, watching him.

He was too worked up, too excited. He would propose to Faith for the second time in less than a week. Granted, the first time hadn't been thought through properly.

But for the first time his life, he'd actually grown afraid. What if she turned him down again? He didn't think he could live without her. The past few days had been pure torture.

Lifting his hand, he glanced at his watch. One p.m.

"So, this is the one, huh?"

Mark eyed his brother for a few seconds. "Yes." He'd never been surer of anything before. "She's the one."

"I hope it works out for you," his kid brother said.

"I hope so, too."

Where was Faith? He restrained from calling her immediately.

Half an hour later with still no Faith, he called her. Something must be wrong. She had never been late for any of their previous appointments; he didn't think she would start now.

But her phone rang without been picked up and he got really worried.

"I have to go," he said to his brother as he headed out.

"What if she shows up?" Tony asked.

"Tell her to wait for me and call me immediately."

For the drive to Lekki, he took all the shortcuts he knew but still didn't seem to get there fast enough. The gate man to the mini complex let him in. When he rang her doorbell, he got no reply. When he asked the gateman about her, he said Faith had left that morning and hadn't returned.

"Faith, where are you?" he muttered under his breath as he headed back to his car.

His phone vibrated in his pocket and he dug it out, thinking it was Faith. No luck. Felix.

"If you're calling to find out what happened at the date, she never showed up," he said when he answered the phone.

"I know," Felix said. "Ebony just told me Faith has gone to Benin."

"What? Why?"

"It's Faith's mother. She's in the hospital."

"Oh, no." His heart raced and he shook his head in denial. "What happened?"

"I don't know the full details except that she's very ill."

"Do me a favour. Please ask Ebony to text me Faith's home address and the name of the hospital her mum's in."

"Okay. What are you going to do?" his brother asked.

"I'm going to Benin."

He hung up and called his travel agent to sort a flight for him. Then he headed home to get what he needed.

An hour later, he sat on the last flight out to Benin. A chauffeured car hire service picked him up from the airport and drove him straight to the hospital.

People waited at the reception area but he didn't see Faith.

"I'm looking for Mrs. Brown," he said to the nurse at the desk.

The woman in white uniform inspected him through her black-rimmed spectacles.

"Who are you to be asking?" she asked.

The way she stared at him, he knew she wouldn't tell him anything if she knew he wasn't a relative, and no way he would come this far without accomplishing his goal.

"She is my mother-in-law. Faith, her daughter, is my fiancée." Not exactly a lie when it would happen sooner or later.

Someone shuffled down the corridor, the sound of their footsteps slow and tired. Mark looked up and saw Faith. Her shoulders were slumped and her hand rubbed her eyes. As if sensing him, she looked up as he walked over to her.

She appeared shocked and confused at seeing him. Didn't she know there was nowhere he'd rather be than beside her, especially at a time like this?

He stopped two steps from her.

"How is your mother?" he asked.

She blinked once. Twice. Her jaw clenched as if she fought to stay calm.

"She's dying, Mark." Her voice came out strangled, her eyes glassy with tears. "My mother is dying.

A tight band of pain squeezed his chest as his heart broke for her and he did the only thing he could. He opened his arms and surprisingly, she stepped into the circle of his embrace.

He held onto her, rubbing her back as she started sobbing, knowing he would do whatever it took to see her laugh again.

***

For the first time since she was a teenager, Faith cried. Really cried. The bawling-like-a-baby-with-a-snotty-nose kind of cry both heart-wrenching to watch yet soul-cleansing.

Considering she hadn't cried in so long and she'd always been able to keep her emotions in check enough not to break down in public ever, she didn't know how she ended up sobbing her eyes out in the reception room of a hospital.

But here she stood in Mark's arms, thoroughly soaking his shirt with tears and snot, the rumbling of his soothing voice and the light strokes of his fingers from her nape down her spine urging her to let go.

Mark.

Perhaps it was seeing him standing there in the middle of the hallway, knowing he'd come here because of her, seeing the concern on his face when she tried to be brave about her mother's illness. Surely, he knew about the fate of City Investments by now and what she'd done.

Finally, in her brain, it clicked.

She could trust him.

Despite everything she did to him. He would always be there for her when it mattered. Really mattered. Like here and now.

Another bout of sobbing erupted within her.

What had she done to deserve him, to deserve such loyalty and devotion, especially when she'd pushed him away at every opportunity?

"It's okay, sweetheart. I'm here for you." His fingers stroked down her back again.
"We'll do whatever it takes to make her better."

She shut her eyes tightly as her sorrow deepened. She believed him. But perhaps it was already too late to save her mother.

She tried to wipe her cheeks with the sleeves of her blouse but Mark pushed a handkerchief into her hand. Somehow, she didn't feel any embarrassment as she wiped her face.

"Is it okay if I speak to the doctor who is attending to her?" Mark asked when she clutched the fabric in her hand.

Her body still leaned against him and for the first time ever, she didn't want to let go of him. "Okay."

Mark seemed to sense her need for closeness because he didn't let go of her. Instead, he guided them to the reception desk, his hand around her waist.

"I would like to speak to the doctor attending to Mrs. Brown," he said to the receptionist.

"I'll find out if he's available," the woman replied.

They stood there while she walked around the desk and disappeared down the corridor.

"What exactly was the diagnosis?" Mark asked.

Faith closed her eyes and swallowed as she fought back another bout of tears.

"Cancer." She had to force the word out of her mouth. "I don't know what to do."

For the first time in her adult life, she didn't have a plan of action. Nothing had prepared her for this.

"Oh, sweetheart." Mark hugged her tighter, his chin leaning on her head.

His words conveyed as much pain as she felt. For the first time in a long time, she was glad she had someone to lean on to and share the load on her shoulders with.

The nurse returned. "The doctor will see you now."

She turned and they followed her with Mark still holding onto her. For the first time, she was seeing the true benefit of their visceral connection. She felt grounded, safe, and secure, as if they could conquer the challenges they faced together.

In the doctor's office, Mark introduced himself as Faith's fiancé. Apart from a quick glance at him, she didn't refute his words. Not important now. They would discuss it later. They sat in separate armchairs though they were still linked as Mark held her hand.

"Mr. Essien," Dr. Adesuwa said. "The prognosis doesn't look good for Mrs. Brown. Unfortunately, the cancer wasn't caught early enough. Her immune system is weakened and the cancer cells have spread."

Hearing the words from the doctor made Faith want to yell at the unfairness of it all. Her mother didn't smoke or drink and she wasn't particularly obese. So why her?

Mark squeezed her hand, giving her a reassuring glance.

"Is there nothing that can be done? Radiotherapy? Chemotherapy? Anything?" he asked.

"I've left a message for one of my colleagues at the LUTH Cancer Centre. I'm waiting to see what he recommends."

Mark nodded, his brow creased as he frowned in thought.

"There's a new Cancer Clinic in Lagos which we helped to fund. I wonder if it is possible to fly her down to Lagos."

"It is possible. But I won't recommend it for another forty-eight hours. I want to let her body get used to the drugs and monitor her progress first. Also, I will need to arrange a nurse to travel with her, if you are happy to foot the bill."

"That is not a problem," Mark said. "I will arrange for a private plane or helicopter to transport her so she can be as comfortable as possible. Just let me know when you think it is possible and I will arrange it."

"Good," the doctor said. "It will make things easier if there was space for her to lie down during the transfer."

"Here's my card." Mark gave him a gold-embossed, black business card. "I would be glad if you can contact me as soon as you know more."

The man took the card and nodded.

After they left the doctor's office, she let go of Mark's hand reluctantly.

"Thank you, Mark, but you should go. It's getting late."

He shook his head, staring at her with those black eyes she could drown in.

"What are you going to do? Where are your dad and brother?" he asked.

"They left already. I was going to spend the night here but Mum told me to go home."

"You should."

"I can't, Mark. I don't want to leave her."

"Then I'm staying with you."

He took her hand and led her to the bench in the reception area. He sat down and pulled her beside him. She tilted her head against his chest as he held her body.

"Why are you doing this?" she asked, overwhelmed by his tender actions. She found it difficult reconciling the man in the boardroom with the one now holding her. He'd hurt her with his bid to buy City and yet, here he sat, ready to suffer discomfort on her behalf. Was he just trying to appease her?

Several breaths later, Mark's forefinger knuckle pushed under her chin. She lifted her head to stare into his face.

"Do you really need me to explain?" he asked.

"Yes, Mark. I need to understand this thing between us. If you're just doing this because you want me to back off from City—"

"Forget City, business. I'm here for you because I love you."

He took a deep breath and looked down at her. His love shone in his eyes.

Mouth flying open, she clutched her chest as her heart thumped so loudly, she swore he could hear its erratic beat. Did she really hear right?

"When it comes to you, I don't care about the business. You can have City if it makes you happy. But I want you in my life. I want to be part of my child's life and not just as an occasional parent, either. I will always be there for you. I want to share everything with you, whether they are troubled moments like this or more happier times ahead."

He huffed out a long breath at the end of his speech, lifting the hair that had fallen on her forehead.

Giddy, tears clogged her eyes but she beamed a smile at him as a glimmer of hope shone into her life. A tear rolled down her face. The pad of his thumb felt soft and warm as it brushed the moisture away.

"Am I really that terrible? Is there no place in your heart for me?"

"Oh, Mark." She choked as she half-laughed, half-cried and buried her face in his chest again. "You're already occupying the entire space."

"What did you say?"

He tilted her head up again.

This time, she smiled up at him. "You launched an aggressive takeover on my heart from the night you kissed me in that bar in Jo'burg. I love you, Mark."

"You do?"

She nodded. "I do."

"So why did you reject me when I asked you to marry me?"

"Well, first of all, you didn't ask me, as I recall. You *demanded* I marry you."

He had the good nature to grimace.

"And moreover, at the time, I thought your business was more important to you than me."

"Okay, you have me there. But for the record, you did insist on keeping business matters separate, and I had planned on doing the proposal thing again properly."

"Really? When?"

"At our lunch date. You were going to get the full works. Candlelight, flowers, champagne, engagement ring, you name it."

"Engagement ring? You bought me an engagement ring?"

"Yes, of course."

"I want to see it."

"Now?" He looked around the reception area. A man dozed in a chair and a nurse sat at the nurses' station.

"Yes, now. Or have you changed your mind?"

"Of course not." He reached for his blazer he'd left over the back of the seat and took out a small box from the pocket.

Faith's head pounded. He'd really bought an engagement ring. She held her breath as he opened it. The most beautiful solitaire diamond sat on a platinum ring.

"Gosh, it's beautiful."

He went down on one knee and took her left hand.

"Faith, you are strong, capable, brilliant, independent, and beautiful. From the first day I saw you sitting in the seminar at that conference in South Africa, I've known that you would be someone special to me. I have achieved things that other men envy me for, but I know without a doubt that my life with be dull and nothing without you. I know you're very capable and you're not a damsel in distress, but if you let me, I'd love to be your knight. To be the one you lean on, the one who worships you, the one who protects you. Let me be that man. Marry me, Faith."

"My knight." She nodded and beamed him a huge smile. "I love the sound of you rescuing me once in a while. Yes, I will marry you."

She extended her fingers and he slipped the ring onto the third one. And then he kissed her like he'd just taken ownership of her and she let him. This time, she was happy to belong and be possessed.

The sound of clapping broke them apart.

"Congratulations to both of you," the nurse said.

"Thank you," they replied in unison.

She lifted her hand, staring at the ring in awe. When did he have time to buy such a beautiful item in the past week?

"When did you buy the ring?" she asked staring up at him.

He had a grin on his face.

"I bought it in New York after I realised I was in love with you."

"Oh my gosh. You mean you had this ring on you that day in the limousine?"

"Yes." His smile resembled pure sin. "I was hoping to take you out to dinner that evening and ask you properly."

"Oh, no." She gasped in embarrassment. "And I told you we were over." Then she remembered. "And I slapped you, on top of all that. And you still want to marry me."

"Yes." He gave a bark of laughter. "But I'm hoping for less grievous bodily harm."

She bit her lip. "I'm sorry about that. Did it hurt?"

She lifted her hand and caressed his cheek.

"Not if you promise to make it up to me sometime." His eyes sparkled with mischief.

"What will I have to do?" she asked tentatively.

"You let me chain you to my kitchen sink."

"Hell, no."

He laughed.

"Oh, well. A guy's got to try."

He leaned down and kissed her again.

CHAPTER SEVENTEEN

Faith clutched her hands on the lap. They trembled. She couldn't remember the last time she'd been so nervous.

"Mark, I'm not sure I'm ready for this. I don't do family very well," she said through a dry throat.

Strong fingers stroked her thigh. "Stop worrying. You'll be fine. It's just my family and you've met them before."

"Yes, the last time I met them, I was just Ebony's friend and Alex's godmother. They are not going to feel the same way when you introduce me as your fiancée."

"Well, Ebony and Felix will be there supporting us. Kola and Tony are easygoing, and my parents are pretty cool."

"But your mum wants you to get married to Wumi. I don't have Wumi's breeding and status."

Mark snorted. "I won't have you referring to yourself as if you were a mare or cow. You are the woman I love. Beautiful, intelligent, and you actually make your own money. You don't need status. You are the next MD of City Investments. That should be good enough for anybody, including my mother."

Faith was stunned by the vehemence of his speech. But she loved that he was passionate about her. She smiled.

"Thank you. That makes me feel much better."

"Good. I am looking forward to finally showing you off to me family. It is well overdue."

The black and gold gilded gate of the Essien mansion opened up and Mark drove his sleek sports car down the drive and parked in an empty car port spot. The carport looked like a showroom for expensive automobiles. She recognised the Porsche Cayenne that belonged to Felix and

Ebony, a Range Rover Sport, and a Bentley Cashmere. Mark's Aston Martin DB9 certainly looked like it belonged there.

He stepped around and opened the door for her. She was stunned to find a super motorbike among the assortment of vehicles on display.

"So who rides the bike in your family?"

"Who else but the family rebel?" Mark said with a smile.

"You mean Tony?" She'd heard Mark refer to his brother as the rebel previously.

"Of course. He nearly gave my mum a heart attack the first time he bought one. But she got used to the fact that he isn't going to give it up."

"A guy after my heart."

Mark frowned. "Don't tell me you are into motorbikes, too?"

"No way. I'm still getting used to the ride of your sport cars. That's fast enough for me. No, I was referring to his rebellion. I know what it feels like to do something against your parents' wishes."

"Well, then the two of you will get on like a house on fire."

They found the rest of the family in the back garden. Felix and Tony were playing table tennis while Ebony and Mark's parents watched and cheered on from the shade of the gazebo. Felix put his bat down on the table and hugged his brother.

"Good to see you, Faith" he said. "How is your mother doing?"

"Much better now that she's seeing a specialist, thanks to Mark."

"It's the least I can do," Mark said and took her hand, giving it a gentle squeeze.

Ebony embraced her while Mark hugged his parents and exchanged pleasantries.

"Mum, Dad, you remember Faith, don't you?"

"Yes," his dad said.

"Isn't she Ebony's friend?" his mum asked.

"Yes, that's correct."

"It's good to see you again, Faith."

"Welcome."

"Thank you." Faith curtsied.

Mark stood next to her and held her hand. "I wanted to bring her here today and formally introduce her to you. We have some news for you. Faith is the woman I'm going to marry, and we are expecting our first child."

"Is that so?" his mother said.

"Well done, son," his father said. "Faith, come and sit down. You are welcome to our family."

His brothers and Ebony hugged both of them and congratulated them, the men thumping Mark's back. They thanked them and settled into their seats next to each other.

"So Faith, tell us about your family. Where are your parents? What do they do?" Mark's mother asked.

Faith's face heated up. She'd been expecting those questions but still felt uncomfortable about answering them. Her family hung in a different league from the Essiens.

"My parents live in Benin City. My father is a mechanic, and my mother is teacher."

The older Essien woman stood up abruptly. "Excuse me. Mark, I need to talk to you now." She walked off towards the house.

Mark patted Faith's hand. "I won't be long," he said and followed after his mother.

Ebony smiled encouragingly at her and Faith swallowed and returned her smile.

"So, how are you parents doing?" Chief Essien asked.

"Not so good. We found out ten days ago that my mother has cancer."

"I'm so sorry to hear that. Is there anything I can do? Where is she being treated?"

"She's already receiving the best care possible thanks to Mark. He arranged to fly her from Benin City to Lagos.

She is in the cancer clinic and the oncologist has diagnosed it as leukaemia, although they are yet to determine the particular subtype to they can start treating it immediately."

Sadness washed over Faith. She only came here because her mother had convinced her to live her life.

"Don't wake up one day and find out that you haven't lived all because you are waiting for the outcome of one plan or the other."

"What about you, Mum? I just can't pretend that you are not in here and very sick."

"My daughter, what will be will be. If God decides this is my time to go and join Him, then I have no quarrel about it. I have lived my life as best as I could. It is now your turn."

Tears misted her eyes. "Excuse me. I need to use the bathroom."

"Do you need me to show you?" Ebony asked.

"No. I remember where it is."

In the house, she was heading down the hallway when she recognised Mark's voice and froze on the spot.

"I love Faith and I want to marry her."

"No! Can't you see she is just a cheap gold digger? A nobody. Her parents are nobodies. She is just trying to trap you with that pregnancy. We can take care of it. Pay her a large amount of money to make her go away."

"Mother, I won't have you talk about her like that. In fact, this conversation is over right now."

Faith didn't have time to move from her spot. The next thing she knew, Mark stood in the hallway staring at her with shock on his face.

But his shock certainly couldn't match hers. His loud, frustrated groan suddenly unfroze her body. Faith ran into the downstairs bathroom and shut the door. Silent tears ran down her face but she ignored them, just like she ignored the banging on the door and Mark's insistence for her to open up.

Mark had never been so livid in his life. He couldn't believe his mother had said those vile things about his fiancée. The worst was that Faith had seemingly heard it all. No amount of knocking on the door had made her open the bathroom after she ran into it.

"What is going on?" his father asked.

Mark swivelled. "Mother doesn't like my choice of wife and said some really unpleasant things, and Faith heard them. Now, she's locked herself into the bathroom and refuses to open the door," he growled and paced.

"Are you sure you heard your mother right?"

"I'm absolutely certain. I believe she used 'cheap gold digger' and 'a nobody' as descriptions of Faith. This is not right, Dad."

"But I was saying the truth," Mrs. Essien said. "The girl is only trying to trap him by getting pregnant."

"If she's a gold digger, then so are you, Mother. At least, she didn't get pregnant for a married man!" Mark's voice was so cold as opposed to the rage boiling inside him.

Everyone around him froze and he heard hisses as people sucked in air sharply. He caught Felix's gaze. His older brother's expression was the 'what the fuck are you doing?' look.

"What did you just say to me?" his mother said.

"Apologise to your mother," his father ordered.

"All I said was the truth. Mother was no better than Faith before she married you. In fact, Faith is in a much better position. She's going to be the next MD of City Investment firm. She doesn't need my money. But I need her. And if she refuses to marry me because of what just happened, I swear I will never forgive Mum."

"I will marry you," a soft voice said behind him.

Mark turned around so fast, his head spun. Faith stood just outside the door to the bathroom. He went to her and gave her a tight hug.

"Sweetheart, I'm so sorry about what you heard. I'm so sorry it upset you. I promise you we don't have to come back to this house until everyone here accepts you."

She pulled back and looked up at his face. "This is your family home, Mark. You can't just ban yourself from coming here."

"Don't you get it? You are the most important person to me. You are going to be my wife, the mother of my child. Anybody who doesn't accept you rejects me. And I reject them in return."

"It hasn't come to that, son."

"I mean it, Mum. If you can't accept Faith, then be ready to wave goodbye to me."

His mother's skin paled and her throat bobbed as she swallowed.

"Look, I'm sorry. I didn't realise you felt so strongly about her. I just thought she was one of your fun-time girls."

Mark put his arms around Faith's shoulders. "She's the real deal, Mum. Are you going to welcome her in as your daughter-in-law?"

"I just have one question for Faith. Do you love my son?"

Faith glanced up at him and then back at his mother.

"I love Mark very much. He has restored my faith in men and shown me that life is for the living. If he lets me, I want to spend the rest of my life paying him back for the wonderful gift of love that he has given me."

"In that case, you are welcome into the Essien family, Faith. Forgive my previous harsh words."

"There's nothing to forgive, Mrs. Essien. You were only trying to protect your son."

"You have to call me Mum. I hope you will look upon me as such."

"Of course, Mum."

"Come on people, dinner awaits."

Giving Faith another tight squeeze, Mark breathed a sigh of relief as they headed into the dining room.

CHAPTER EIGHTEEN

"Mr. Petersen is here now," the receptionist announced through the intercom sitting on the boardroom table.

"Send him in," Faith replied and pressed the button to switch it off.

Her shoulders lifted as she heaved a sigh and muttered under her breath, "The game is on."

The boardroom door opened and Kris Petersen walked in dressed in one of his trademark flamboyant suits. This time, a navy one with gold embroidery.

"Good afternoon, Mr. Petersen," she greeted, extending her hand for a shake.

The man ignored her hand and shoved a newspaper at her, instead. "What is this I read about you and Mark Essien—"

His eyes widened as he caught sight of the man standing by the windows overlooking the city.

"Essien!"

"Petersen," Mark replied. "I can't say it's good to see you, but what you read is quite correct this time. Ms. Brown and I are soon to be married."

Petersen's glare shifted from Mark to Faith. He scanned her body.

"And yes, we are expecting a baby together." Mark strode across the room and stood beside her. She stood tensely and her hand trembled. He reached for it. With a gentle squeeze, he held onto her and gave her a smile.

He worried about her. She hadn't been sleeping very well as she continued to fret over her sick mother despite the fact that the woman was doing better at the Cancer

Clinic in Lagos than she'd been a few weeks ago in Benin City.

She had wanted to meet Petersen alone. But Mark had insisted on being here. He knew how mean and dirty the man could get, and there was no way he was going to leave her alone with him.

Faith looked up at him and gave him a small, still tense smile.

"Mr. Petersen, please sit down and I'll explain," she said and gave the man an encouraging smile.

Petersen settled in one of the chairs on the opposite end of the table. "I don't want him here. This is a confidential business meeting."

"That's not going to happen," Mark replied as he sat in the chair next to Faith and stretched his legs out.

"I have a contract with Miss Brown and it doesn't involve you, Essien." The way the man said Essien made it sound like a dirty word.

"Wrong again—"

Faith covered Mark's hand on the table with hers, stilling his words.

"What Mark is trying to say is that I'm going to back out of our deal. I am cancelling the contract."

"Why?" The man looked flabbergasted.

"Mark made me a better deal."

"Whatever deal he made you, I'll double the offer."

Faith's eyes widened but she remained outwardly calm. "I'm afraid you misunderstand me. Mark's offer is not only financial. He is offering me something no other man can give me."

Petersen frowned. "What's that?"

"Himself."

Petersen's face turned red and he looked ready to explode. "But you forget that you cannot pull out of the deal for another eighteen months. Or you lose everything."

"Mr. Petersen, I was hoping I could appeal to your humanity considering the extenuating circumstances. I'm dealing with the stress of my mother who is critically ill in hospital and, added to the hormonal influence of my first pregnancy, I've decided that taking on the demanding role of MD at this time will not be good for City Investment nor for your investment. The merger with Apex Financials will provide City with sure-handed security for the near future while I adjust to the unexpected changes around me. As you are a shareholding member of the Apex Holdings board, I thought you would appreciate this decision."

"No," Petersen replied. "If you wanted my understanding, you should have come to me first instead of getting in bed with the Essiens. If you want to walk away from the deal, you do it at your own loss. I retain City."

"Aren't you jumping the gun, Petersen?" Mark asked. "City is not yours to retain."

"What nonsense. I signed a contract with Miss Brown and Mr. Okolo accepted her proposal."

"That may be so. But Mr. Okolo never signed a contract with you nor with Miss Brown. And according to the papers in my possession—" Mark pulled out a sheaf of papers from his brown leather briefcase, "—he signed on the dotted line to the original offer I made him."

"Miss Brown, tell me this isn't so." Petersen pushed back his chair and stood.

"Mark is telling the truth. The merger has been agreed to by Mr. Okolo and contracts exchanged."

"You haven't heard the last of this. You will be hearing from my lawyers."

"Before you run off and start litigations' proceedings, you should also consider what EFCC will do about your insider trading activities."

Petersen's eyes narrowed. "Are you threatening me, Essien?"

"You can take it as you wish." Mark stood and braced his hands on the table as he eyeballed the man. "But I warn you, if you do anything that upsets the wellbeing of my wife-to-be, I will make it my mission to make your life a misery. You got away with threatening Ebony; you won't do the same with Faith. If you want a fight, pick on me."

The man glared from Mark to Faith and back again. Then he huffed and walked out of the room, slamming the door behind him. The walls shook.

Mark walked to the door and locked it. He turned around and found Faith with her head in her hands. His chest tightened. If someone had told him over a year ago when he'd first met Faith that he would be madly in love with her and would do just about anything simply to make her happy, he would have laughed out loud.

But here he stood. Ready to take on the world for her. He'd already challenged his mother and won. He'd taken on Petersen and remained ready for anyone else who would seek to hurt her. If he could wave a wand and make her mother's illness disappear, he would. As it was, he was already paying for the best medical care that Nigeria could provide.

He strode back to where she sat, wrapped his arms around her torso, and lifted her to sit on the table.

"That went well," she said as she looked up at him with a small smile on her face. But she couldn't hide the tiredness on her features.

He gathered her closer and tucked her head under his chin. "Don't worry about Petersen. His bark is harsher than his bite. He is smart enough to know that I'm a fierce opponent to cross. Unfortunately for him, I don't have Felix's sentimentality. I will ruin Petersen if he does anything against you. And I won't lose any sleep over it."

Faith leaned her head back. "I'm glad I'm no longer on your wrong side. Now I see why none of the other investors wanted to go against you. I was really surprised when Petersen volunteered to fund me. I suspected something wasn't right, but I was more interested in getting the funding and beating you. I'm sorry."

"Hey, don't be. You did what you thought was right. You couldn't have known that Petersen had an ulterior motive."

"But why does he seem to have a grudge against the Essiens? What did you all do to him?"

"Honestly, I don't know what the man's problem is. I only really started taking notice of him when he raised the notion of replacing Felix as head of Apex Private Bank at a board meeting. Afterwards, Ebony's ex-fiancé confessed that Petersen had used him to get information about Felix and Ebony and used it to try to blackmail them. The man just seems to have it in for the Essiens. But we are up for it. We've beaten him before. We will keep on beating him."

"Some people are just weird."

"Tell me about it. But enough about Petersen. I'm more interested in turning you into an Essien."

He leaned down and captured her lips in a soul-searing kiss. He poured all his love into it, wanting her to know he would always be there for her. His body had other needs, though, the urge to drive into her warm flesh riding his veins. He broke the kiss, remembering where he was. Faith always wanted to keep things professional in the office and there were people beyond the walls and door. He needed to respect her boundaries.

"Love me," she said in a low voice that threatened to floor him.

"I love you, sweetheart. Always," he replied, meeting her gaze and nearly getting lost in her brown eyes.

"I know, Mark. I love you, too." Her gaze struck him as intense, conveying more than her words. "But I want you to make love to me."

"Here? Now?"

"Yes. My mother accused me of being too afraid. Of not living. And her illness has made me reassess my life. If something happened to me, I want to go knowing that I lived my life to the fullest. That I didn't let fear or rules overshadow me."

"Nothing is going to happen to you. I won't let it. We are going to have a long life together." His grip on her arms tightened.

"I know. And I want to live a full and long life with you. But I also want to be spontaneous, to borrow a leaf from your book every now and then. Right now, I want you to give me one of those things no other man can give me. You. Will you give me what I want?"

Her smile looked so coquettish, all of Mark's arguments disappeared. If she wanted him here and now, no way he was going to say no.

"Yes," he replied, and brushed his lips against hers.

EPILOGUE

Faith couldn't believe the spectacle. The Essiens had descended on Benin City. Her family compound had come alive. Music blasted from speakers as a live band played hi-life. Colourful Tarpaulin canopies on metal stilts protected the visitors seated beneath from the harsh afternoon sunshine.

Faith swung her hips to the music as she danced, her soul filled with joy. Her hair had been styled in an updo and decorated with an intricate beaded tiara. Chunky, coral bead necklaces weighed down her neck. Her body had been swathed in a burgundy lace and organza wrapper that looked like a sleeveless gown to the untrained eye. Over her head sat a cream lace veil designed so that the groom didn't not see her until he had paid the dues.

Women led her with her friends behind. Ebony followed closely with Stella and three other girls including Tari, Mark's cousin. The girls were all dressed in matching uniform outfits in cream and burgundy, the theme colours for her traditional wedding.

Traditional wedding. Faith allowed the words to play in her mind. She never knew a time would come when she would relish those words when associated with her. As an adult, she had always rejected the idea of getting married. When her girlfriends got excited about getting married, she'd always been nonchalant about it, choosing instead to focus on her career.

Now her career was taking a back seat as she focused on making a family with Mark.

Mark.

She glanced across the driveway of her family compound to where her soon-to-be husband was seated almost regally in his traditional Efik outfit with his father and brothers flanking him.

His gaze had been on her as soon as he had stepped out of the house. Her skin had come alive as it always did when he was looking at her. Through the veil, she could see the intensity of his gaze and it took her breath away. She smiled shyly and looked away as her face heated up.

She had never been one for public declarations or displays. But you couldn't get any more public than a traditional wedding. When your family and friends stood by and watched you submit and declare to take a man as your husband. But she knew Mark loved her. He'd shown her that men were capable of deep love and that she deserved that love.

The girls in her entourage led her to the marquee where her father was seated with his kinsmen. The smile on her father's face was the best she'd seen for years. She'd never known the rift with her father could be repaired, but after her mother's hospitalisation and her subsequent engagement to Mark, he had mellowed. They hadn't had an argument and he now allowed her to stay in the house anytime she visited Benin.

As a group, they stopped in front of where the Essiens sat. The lead woman spoke in Edo and her mother interpreted it in English. She was asking Mark to pay some money so he could see his bride. Mark stood and gave the woman some Naira notes. He was then allowed to lift the veil off her head and everyone cheered.

The music restarted and the rest of the Essien brothers stood and started spraying Naira notes over her body like confetti. The act was supposed to bless her with prosperity. Faith's friends picked up the Naira notes and put them in a bag.

Faith was led to a chair opposite where Mark sat and settled into it and the wedding procedure commenced. Butterflies fluttered in her stomach.

Mark beamed at her from across the courtyard. Her nerves settled.

They were going to have a great life together.

227

OUT NOW!

RIDING REBEL, THE ESSIEN SERIES, BOOK 3

Seen as the rebel Essien, Tony has always felt like an outsider. With a daredevil lifestyle, he's more at home in leathers than in a suit, and more likely to be seen gracing the red carpets at a movie premiere with a starlet draped on his arms than in a boardroom. Still, he's determined to prove himself to his family and build a successful movie business. Spotting Rita Dike at an event, he sees the potential star of his new movie and his next pleasure conquest.

Rita is a journalist looking for her big break. When she inherits the journal of her late best friend who claims Tony is not an Essien, she spots the perfect scoop. Her acting classes come in handy when she has to pose as an actress to get closer to Tony. Succumbing to the charms of dark and brooding Tony might just be the only way to get through the close ranks of the Essien family.

But as she gets closer to the truth, Rita risks losing the riding rebel who's raided her heart. Can love heal hearts or will deceit break them?

OTHER BOOKS BY LOVE AFRICA PRESS

Healing His Medic by Nana Prah

Queer and Sexy Collection Volume 1

His Defiant Princess by Nana Prah

His Inherited Princess by Empi Baryeh

His Captive Princess by Kiru Taye

CONNECT WITH US

Facebook.com/LoveAfricaPress

Twitter.com/LoveAfricaPress

Instagram.com/LoveAfricaPress

www.loveafricapress.com

www.ingramcontent.com/pod-product-compliance
Lightning Source LLC
Chambersburg PA
CBHW050354190726

48284CB00007BB/2280